CLAIMING
GEORGINA
TATE

CLAIMING GEORGIA TATE

GIGI AMATEAU

WALKER BOOKS

This is a work of fiction. Names, characters, places and incidents are either products of the author's imagination or, if real, are used fictitiously.

First published 2006 by Walker Books Ltd
87 Vauxhall Walk, London SE11 5HJ

2 4 6 8 10 9 7 5 3 1

Text © 2005 Gigi Amateau
Cover photograph © 2005 Chris Cole / Getty Images

"Vespers" is taken from *When We Were Very Young*. Text by A. A. Milne
© the Trustees of the Pooh Properties. Published by Egmont UK Ltd and
used with permission.

This book has been typeset in Bembo

Printed and bound in Great Britain by Cox & Wyman Ltd, Reading, Berkshire

British Library Cataloguing in Publication Data:
a catalogue record for this book is available from the British Library

ISBN-13: 978-1-84428-155-8
ISBN-10: 1-84428-155-8

www.walkerbooks.co.uk

To drag queens and granddaddies,
for their amazing healing powers

PART ONE

The dolphins play close by, and in my mind I swim with them. We leap in threes, and I am in the middle. They go under and take me with them. They smile at me and I smile back. We don't ever have to talk with words. We jump and circle and splash each other, and we laugh hard without making a single sound. When they go away, swimming up the beach, I want to go, too.

CHAPTER ONE

Sometimes he goes out so deep with me that the water is over my head. Then he picks me up and holds me close to him—too close for me, but we are so far out that I get scared and can't let go. In the city pool at home, I am a good swimmer. I don't even mind going down to the deep end sometimes, but it's different being here in the ocean.

His wife, Sissy, has frosted blond hair. She is the prettiest woman I have ever seen. She doesn't swim or make sandcastles. She sleeps on the blanket while my father and I are in the water.

I am wearing my purple two-piece bathing suit with white flowers all over the top and bottom. I am staying with my father for the summer. Even though I don't know him so well, he makes me call him Daddy. Daddy picked me up from Nana and Granddaddy Tate's, and we drove all the way from Mississippi to Jacksonville, Florida, where he and Sissy live. As soon as we walked in the door, Sissy started complaining about feeling cooped up. So we packed up again and drove here to Panama City.

I don't really remember much about my daddy before now. He moved away when my mama died, and I'm real glad that I don't live with him all the time. Sometimes I'll get a card at Christmas or on what he thinks is my birthday. Nana always asks me if the card has any money in it. It never does.

"You sure are a pretty little girl" was all my father said when he first saw me at Nana's. I just kept on looking at the ground, hoping he'd go away, until Nana poked me in the ribs. Then I said, "Thank you."

"How old are you now, ten?"

"No, sir, I'm twelve."

I could tell Nana really didn't want me to go with him. Nana has never really liked my daddy, or his family. They are what she calls *social*—that means they drink. And I certainly didn't want to go, either. But she and I already had a big fuss about it—more than one fuss, in fact.

In my mind, it would all be a whole lot easier on everybody if my daddy just stayed away. But Nana and Granddaddy Tate say he's got rights. If you ask me, which nobody does, they don't want to make a big stink about me going with him because they're scared of him. I think he must be one of those bullies who gets his way by threatening people who are nicer than he is.

"Please don't make me go. I'll miss the Fourth of July. I'll miss revival."

Revival is when we go to church out in the country, every night of the week. It always starts right after the Fourth of July, and the very last day is called homecoming. That's when everybody makes their best dishes: fried chicken, ham, potato salad, three-bean salad and about a hundred other salads, and at least as many cakes and pies. Last year, there was a guest preacher from Corinth who I thought bragged a little bit too much about his own suffering. Homecoming is also when all of the families who used to go to church in the country but moved to town come back for one night.

My granddaddy has the main church in town, but he also has three little churches out in the country parts of the county: New Life, New Hope, and New Covenant. They all take turns with him so that at least they get a preacher sometimes. Granddaddy also goes visiting the country Presbyterians when they need some counseling or are in the hospital. The revival this summer, which I will miss, is at New Life. New Life always has the best food.

Anyway, I knew it was no use fussing anymore with Nana. So here I am on vacation with my daddy, who's basically a stranger.

What I do love about the ocean is how some spots are warmer than the bathtub, but some spots are ice cold, like when you first jump into a swimming pool. I never know when one of those hot or cold spots is coming up, and it always surprises me. Right now, even though I am with my daddy in the water, I feel like I am alone. I wish I were brave enough to let go of him and swim off to the dolphins.

As his hand slips into my bathing suit bottom, he asks, "Do you like for me to hold you like this?" I don't know if he means with his hand there, or if he means do I like that he is keeping me from drowning in the ocean. If I say no, he might drop me. I don't say anything and close my eyes.

In my mind, I beg the dolphins to come get me, but soon they are so far down the beach that I can only remember how close they once were. I am glad when Sissy tries to call us out of the water. I open my eyes but his hand is still in there. He doesn't take it out right away; we bounce in the ocean for a little longer.

Finally, we go back to the blanket. Sissy is smoking.

My daddy is smoking, too, and cigarette butts are piled up all around. Nobody smokes at home. Everyone smokes here. Daddy and I sit together in the sand and build a great big sandcastle with a moat around it. His hands are big and hairy, and the sand drizzles out of his fingers into whatever kind of curlicue he wants. The sand doesn't curl when it comes out of my fingers. I will say one thing for my daddy: he builds the fanciest sandcastles I have ever seen. The entire time, that cigarette is hanging out of his mouth until it is just an ash. Then he lights another one.

Sissy is mad about something. Her hands are on her hips and she has stomped off toward the room. My daddy must be mad, too, because he has stomped off toward the ocean. They have left me here at the blanket, alone. I am happy to be by myself for a while. I decide to make an extra-fancy castle, the way I want to make it, with lots of little towers surrounding the moat. It is beginning to look about right when he comes back to get me.

"Come on. Come on with me," he says in a way that sounds like I will be bugging him if I do.

"No, I think I'll just stay right here and finish my sandcastle," I say back, hoping that he will be happy to walk along the beach without me.

"Goddammit, I said to come on with me. Now, get your ass up." He has one of those looks like he is going to pop me good. I get up.

He starts telling me why Sissy is mad, even though I don't really care. It's because he lost all of their money out of his swimming trunks while we were deep in the water. Then he says Sissy thinks that if I hadn't been with them, he wouldn't have lost the money, and plus, they wouldn't be spending so much.

I don't know how they are supposedly spending so much just because I am here. Nana bought me my bathing suit, and I have enough other clothes to last the week. Granddaddy Tate even gave me fifty dollars before I left, but I don't want to give it to them. I'll admit, they did buy me a navy blue baseball cap that says *Panama City* in fancy white letters. But since we have been here, Sissy has bought two new bathing suits, a sun hat, a thirty-dollar pair of sunglasses, a pair of white hot pants, and little souvenirs for a bunch of people at the bar where she works. Plus, she calls up and eats dinner from restaurants every night. I eat pimento cheese sandwiches or other stuff that we brought with us. So I just would like to know how they are spending so much money because of me.

If Nana were here, she would say to ask God to help with the lost money. So that's what I do. I hope that if God helps me find the money, everything will be fine. I whisper, "Please let me find the money, please let me find the money, please let me find the money," over and over again. Suddenly, there is a twenty-dollar bill floating beside my leg. I can't believe it. I rub my eyes hard to be sure I'm not just making this up, and I'm not: it is really there. I ask God to help me find the others. I end up finding three twenty-dollar bills, but even that is barely enough to make him feel better. When I tell him that I just prayed to God and there it was, he laughs and says, "Now you owe God big time."

CHAPTER TWO

The room we are staying in has a little kitchen in it, with a stove, a refrigerator, and a sink. Sissy is cooking grilled cheese sandwiches, and smoke is filling up the whole place. She is crying and smoking cigarettes and waving her arms around.

I want to call Nana, but it will be hard to talk with Sissy so upset and my equally upset daddy trying to calm her down. He shows her the money, and he says he found it in the ocean. She throws the grilled cheese into the trash. "Take me out to dinner. I didn't come to the beach to wait on you or her." I can feel her looking at the back of my head, and I'm pretty sure that I am the "her." I am also for certain sure that she hasn't waited on me even once. She stomps off again, and this time he follows her into the bedroom. They are in there for a long time, long enough for me to start getting really hungry.

In the icebox there is regular cheese, pimento cheese, jelly, Coke, beer, milk, and hot dogs. It is getting dark, and I know that if I don't eat now, they might try to make me go straight to bed when they come out. I take six crackers and fold three pieces of cheese into six pieces of cheese—one for each cracker. I pour a big glass of milk. Drinking the milk so late will probably make me wet the bed, but that's okay for now. I'll bring a towel with me, so if I do, I can just lay the towel over the pee and not wake anyone up. I know I am too old to wet the bed, and nobody besides Nana, Granddaddy Tate, and my best friend, Ginger, even knows that sometimes I still do. Last year, Nana took me to the doctor to see if there was something wrong with my body that I can't hold it through the night. There is nothing wrong, and I'm supposed to grow out of it soon.

I eat the crackers and think how nice it is to be alone. I remember how I felt this afternoon on the beach before we started looking for the money. There is something easy about being alone and deciding what to do and how to do it. Then again, if I think about being by myself too much, I get scared. Like what if they never came out? How would I ever get back to Nana and Granddaddy Tate? I wonder if Nana knows exactly how to get here and how long it would take. I try not to think too much. Not thinking too much makes it kind of fun to fix my own supper, even if it is just crackers and cheese.

When the bedroom door finally opens, he comes out alone. "Get your shoes on. We're going to pick up some dinner. Have you eaten yet?"

Something awful happens inside me and I say, "Yes, sir," even though it was only crackers and I am still hungry. And he believes me. He doesn't ask what I had, or where I got it, or if I'm still hungry. I put on my shoes, and we drive to a restaurant down the street to pick up spaghetti and bread and salad and cheesecake that he has already ordered for Sissy and himself. It all sounds good to me, except the salad, but I know I am not going to get any of it.

When we get back, he takes everything into the bedroom and comes back out for his cigarettes and two beers. I am not brave enough to tell him that I'm still hungry, but after he disappears again, I am brave enough to pick up the phone to call Nana. When I hear her voice, I burst into tears and ask to come home.

"Put your father on the phone," Nana answers me.

"No, I can't. He's not in here right now. He's in the back, and I don't think I can go in there."

"Georgia Tate, you say you want to come home. If that's what you want, I need to talk to your daddy right now to make arrangements."

"Nana, could you please make arrangements without me having to go get him right now?"

Maybe Nana hears something in my voice, or maybe Nana hears something inside herself telling her to get me home quickly. All of a sudden it's like she understands everything that has happened without me having to even tell her.

"Georgia Tate, whatever it is, I will take care of it." When her voice gets all soft, it just comes pouring out of me, all of it does. The way he was touching me, the smoking, the swearing, and how sick I am of pimento cheese sandwiches. I am sobbing and whispering and begging Nana, "Please, come now, I want to be home."

"Shhh, shhh . . . Granddaddy and I will be there before suppertime tomorrow. I'll call your father later tonight after you've gone to sleep. Okay, sweet child?"

My granddaddy always calls me dolly. Nana always calls me sweet child, or Georgia Tate, except when she is angry with me. Then she calls me either just Georgia or Georgia Jamison. My full name is Georgia Tate Jamison. My middle name, Tate, is Nana and Granddaddy's last name. When Nana is mad, she leaves the Tate part out and calls me the two names that are from my daddy's family. My daddy's name is Rayford Jamison, but I was named after his mama. She is named Georgia, too. She and her husband, my other grandparents, the Jamisons, also live in Ripley, Mississippi, the same town I live in with Nana and Granddaddy Tate. They are Methodists who belong to Ripley Methodist, but they don't go to church. I pretty much never see them. Well, the truth is that I see them often. I mean, I know who they are, and they know who I am. When we bump into each other in town, we all speak, and they always say how big I am getting. But I don't ever visit them or even call them by name, because it seems awkward to call them Mr. or Mrs. Jamison, and even more awkward to call them Grandmother or Granddaddy. I feel more happy about the Tate part of my name than the other parts, since it keeps me related to Nana and Granddaddy.

One time when Nana left the Tate part out was when I asked her if she had any more pictures of my daddy. She said she didn't have even one. Well, she surely did, because I had it in my hand, and I said, "Yes, you do, Nana."

I didn't even get the sentence out of my mouth before Nana exploded and said, "Georgia Jamison, shut your mouth right now." Then she popped me hard on the lips, so I just dropped the picture of my mama and daddy both holding me when I was brand-new. I dropped it right at her feet and ran to my room.

Poor Nana felt real bad, like it was her fault. But it wasn't all her fault. I was trying to make her sore. It worked, but I hadn't really expected her to haul off and smack me. When she came into my room later, she set the picture right on top of my pillow and said, "Sweet child, this is the only picture I have of your daddy. You may have it." She did not actually say "Georgia Tate, sorry for popping you," but I think that's what she meant.

Right now I am reading Nana the telephone number to the hotel where we are staying, and then I say, "Okay, I'm going to sleep right now. I love you, Nana."

I decide that if I am going home tomorrow, I need to be clean and fresh. So I draw my own bath. Usually Nana does that for me, even though she always says, "You're big enough to do this yourself," while she's doing it. The bath water is a little bit too cold—I'm nervous about handling the hot water by myself. I guess I should be getting old enough to do it on my own, though. When I don't want to take a full bath, Nana says, "Just take a sponge." That's her country way of saying wash yourself without getting all the way into the tub. So that's what I do now, take a sponge bath.

The parts that Nana says get most dirty are my neck,

my face, my underarms, my bottom, and my "set-tee." That's what Nana calls my privates—my set-tee. That is the part that he touched in the ocean, so I wash it extra good and put on a pair of the brand-new white panties that Nana bought me for this trip. After my sponge bath, I try to get all of the tinkle out of my body because I do not want to wet the bed and go home smelling like pee.

Nana always tells me to find the good in all things. I lie in the bed and try to find all of the good things about this week. It is good that I got better at swimming, good that I found the money, good that by this afternoon my curlicues worked just like I like them, and good that I am going home.

CHAPTER THREE

I am thinking that today is the best day ever. Everyone is at our house for the Fourth of July. This year is special because it's the two-hundredth anniversary of our country and the entire world is celebrating the bicentennial. Every year we have the whole family over on Independence Day, but this year, there are a lot more fireworks and decorations. My cousins from Memphis are here; Aunt Sarah and my cousins from Florence, too. Aunt Mazel from Moulton is here, also. Nana even said I could invite Ginger over. Ginger couldn't come, on account of having to visit her daddy; she had to be with him over the holiday.

The other special thing about this year is that we're electing a new president. Everybody's talking about it. My granddaddy wants Jimmy Carter to win, and I do, too. He seems like a kind man who really listens to people. Everybody else, including Nana, wants to keep President Ford. Nana says we should give him a decent chance. Aunt Mazel won't say how she's voting, but I'm thinking she wants Jimmy Carter, because she says he is a God-fearing man. I know for a fact that she likes God-fearing people of all kinds.

Upstairs in the bathtub is where Granddaddy Tate put the watermelon for us to eat after dark. I helped him fill the tub with cold water, and we put in a couple of big bags of ice from the filling station to cool it down for when we've finished eating dinner. Every now and then, Granddaddy and I go upstairs and roll the watermelon over so it gets cold all the way through. It is so hot today that it would feel good to be the watermelon right about now, or at least to jump in there with it.

Aunt Mazel is my favorite person to see from a long way away. She is so perfect, but not in the prissy, going-to-church kind of way. Perfect more like sitting on the screened porch while it's raining hard outside. She is just easy and soft and beautiful. When she is here, I have to make myself not follow her around every little minute. I would do it if I didn't pay good attention to my manners. Nana also pays good attention to my manners. Most of the time, Nana only has to give me that certain look and I know she means "Go play." Sometimes I don't look at Nana on purpose, so she can't give me the look. That way I have a little bit longer with Aunt Mazel before Nana says something out loud.

I've known Aunt Mazel my whole life, but I never noticed her hand until today. We held hands for the group picture on the porch, and I felt that she has no thumb. I searched for it with my own thumb, because it's not right to hold a hand and not grip the thumb. But it's not there. I really want to ask her about it, but I can feel the look I would get from Nana if I did. I'll ask Nana about it later, after Aunt Mazel goes back home.

She is staying with us for a while, at least a whole week. So, for today, while everybody is here, I am trying not to be greedy by hogging her. It's hard to do, because she acts like I am her favorite person, too. She asks about school and asks am I excited about next year. She even asks about Ginger: "How is that fiery girlfriend of yours?" She doesn't call Ginger by name, but that's who she is talking about for certain.

I can't say that Nana is real happy that Ginger is my best friend. Sometimes, I actually think Nana is especially *un*happy about it. If Ginger were a Presbyterian, or a Baptist like Nana was before she married Granddaddy Tate, then Nana might be more accepting of our friendship. But Ginger and her mom go to the Church of Christ. Also, they used to live in a trailer. Now, though, they live in a nice little house on the same road we live on, but a bit closer to Booneville. Nana always makes a point of calling Ginger's house the Habitat House, because that's how they got it built, through the Habitat for Humanity. When they were building it, Ginger and her mama and the other kids worked on it, too. Nana would not work on it, even though I worked on it a lot.

It embarrassed me that Nana didn't come with me, because it made it so obvious that she didn't like me being friends with Ginger. The second time I helped out, Nana at least brought over some angel food cake that she made for everyone to have with their lunches. She didn't stay long; she held the cake out and said, "The house is coming along real well, Mrs. Parsons. Well, here's some angel food cake. I thought you all might like something sweet after lunch." Nana is the only person I know who never says "y'all." She always says "you all." Ginger's mama was real nice to Nana and even offered to show her through the house, but Nana hurried off. That was good, because I wasn't feeling very friendly toward her at that moment.

Ginger and I were busy mixing concrete for the back patio, anyway.

Another reason I think Nana doesn't like Ginger is because she is thirteen, which Nana thinks is too old for me. Also, Ginger is big-chested but doesn't wear a bra. Nana has already started making me wear a bra, even though I am nowhere near as developed as Ginger. Even when I go fishing I have to wear it. Today, when Granddaddy and I were on our way to the pond, Nana called me back real sharp, like I had forgotten to make the bed. "Georgia Tate, come here a minute."

When I got up to her, she whispered, "Get inside and put your brassiere on."

"But I'm only going fishing. I don't need it."

"Yes, you do, too. The only time you don't need it on is at night, when you go to sleep."

"Even in the shower?" I said that real smarty-pants-like, and I thought she was going to pop me. "Okay," I said, and ran in before she could reach me.

Anyway, my chest is really just two little bumps. I sure do cover up those bumps good with my training bra, or *brassiere,* as Nana says. If mine are bumps, then Ginger's are mountains. She calls them titties. To me, that just sounds bad. So I say "chest," as in, "My chest is growing, but not as fast as Ginger's."

Ginger is right odd about her body, meaning she is not real private or embarrassed of anyone seeing any part of her. One day when I was at her house—not the Habitat House but the old house, which was really a trailer—Ginger said, "Watch this." And I did. I watched her closely, because you never know what's next with her. She took off her shirt; of course, there was no bra under there, nothing holding those mountains back. She stretched out in the middle of the floor and put her turtle on top of her chest—on her titties, to be exact about it—and she just hooted out loud about the turtle crawling across the Titty Mountains. The turtle seemed to be having a good time, and her chest even looked like mountains, but with nipples on top instead of snow. Well, what else could I do except laugh?

Only Ginger—that's why I could only laugh. She didn't see anything bad or wrong, like Nana would have. She was just more or less using what she had available to her to have a good time. And she was trying something new—that's Ginger, too, always just trying new things. I like that in a friend.

I don't tell Aunt Mazel about the Titty Mountains, but I do tell her about everything else fun that we did this year, and also about how I am happy that my teacher from last year, Mrs. Lawrence, will be moving up with us.

"Do you remember any of your teachers?" I ask her.

"Well, we all had the same teacher for every grade. In my school, there were fifteen students in one room, all the way from real young to high school. The older ones taught the younger ones, so the teacher didn't have to worry with all the children at once. One year, the county ran out of money to pay our teacher's salary, so we only went to school until Christmas. We got to stay home the rest of that school year, although I'd rather have been in class. At home, we made quilt after quilt, and I got to be real good at sewing and cooking and making butter. Mama and Daddy found extra chores to keep us busy enough that school would have been the vacation."

I wonder if she still had her thumb then. I know the thumb has been gone a long time, because nobody talks about it and never has as far back as I can remember. If it had happened not too long ago, I'm sure I would be hearing about it regularly, as I like to listen to Nana's end of Saturday phone calls. For example, Aunt Mazel is ninety-five years old. And already, every weekend when Nana and Aunt Sarah talk, they spend at least five minutes going on about how only five more years to go before Aunt Mazel is one hundred.

When Nana calls Aunt Sarah and the other relatives every Saturday, they all talk about the exact same new stories for months at a time, and sometimes even for a year or longer. Like the time Jim, who is older than me

CHAPTER FOUR

When I walk into the kitchen to help fix lunch, I hear my aunt Sarah quizzing Nana about why I am home. So I just stop and hide in the dining room, where I can hear but they can't see me. Nana generally gets on me about eavesdropping, so right now I try to be real quiet and only breathe when I need to.

"I thought Georgia Tate was spending the whole summer with her daddy," says Aunt Sarah.

"She was. Now she's not. Tate and I drove down and picked her up early—he's not fit to be with her."

Granddaddy's first name is Aaron and his middle name is Samuel, but Nana just calls him Tate. She is the only wife I have ever known who calls her husband by just his last name. Even when she is kissing him good night, she just says, "G'night, Tate," and pecks him on the forehead, just like she kisses me good night on the forehead.

"Lucy, what happened?"

I am holding my breath and praying that, for once, Nana doesn't tell Aunt Sarah the whole story. Nana almost always tells all the details that she knows, but this time my mind is pleading with her not to tell. I don't think I could ever face Aunt Sarah again, plus Aunt Sarah has a big mouth and would just blab to everybody.

"Sarah, I can't talk about it. I didn't even tell Tate. I just said, 'We need to get Georgia Tate home.' He nodded straightaway and said, 'I'll go up to the filling station and get gas. You be ready when I get back.' That's why I love him; he's a good man and he listens to me."

I am glad to start breathing again for two reasons—one because Nana didn't tell Aunt Sarah, and two because she didn't tell my granddaddy. I have been feeling right embarrassed around him, thinking of his knowing what my daddy did and all.

"Well, I'm surprised he let you take her back. If I remember, he was never the easiest fellow to get along with."

"It did get kind of ugly. He's threatening to go to court for custody of her. Georgia Tate doesn't know about that, and if I can help it, she won't ever know about it. I don't believe there's a court in the world that would give him custody."

Whatever custody is, it sounds like something I certainly do need to know about, so I just walk in the kitchen like I was on my way, anyway, and I say, "What's custody, Nana?" It must be something terrible, because Nana's face turns whiter than corn.

"Don't worry about that right now, Georgia Tate. Come on and help me and your aunt Sarah with the hush puppies."

I stand in the kitchen, next to Nana, in between her and Aunt Sarah. Nana smells like sweat and cornmeal. Whenever she comes in from the garden, she smells like this. I love especially to garden with Nana, and I know all about every plant in our garden: okra, beans, butter beans, corn, green peppers, squash, field peas, string beans, cucumbers, and watermelon. It's hard for me to tell the difference between cucumbers and watermelon until I can see the actual fruit. Oh, and strawberries; we had so many this year that I just sat down in them and ate and ate and never even made a dent in how many we had.

Nana always sings while she works in the garden. And

she can sure pick some weeds. Some days, that's what she does for two or three straight hours—she picks little teeny weeds that I don't even see at first. When we go out to pick beans or peas, Nana lets me wear her old pink apron with the three pockets in the front. That apron is so old that I have never felt anything softer. We put different vegetables in each pocket until all of the pockets are full, and then we sit at the kitchen table to get everything ready for dinner.

The field peas are my favorite to shell because by the time they are all shucked, the bowl is like a little bitty bathtub full of peas. My hands just love the feel of it. I always ask to do the peas.

Being in the garden with Granddaddy is a lot less work than it is with Nana. He mostly just wanders around showing me where deer or rabbits or moles have been. He likes to listen to all the birds, too. When we actually see a mole, or most often mole tunnels, he goes and tells Nana because she is so good at killing them. Granddaddy is too sweet a man to kill a mole just for acting like a mole. But that Nana, she gets the hoe out and goes to town on it, and then after she's killed it, she lays the dead mole out in the carport like it's a big prize.

Every day, she marks on the calendar how many moles she has killed. Like now, it's the beginning of July, and she has already killed ten moles this month. That is more than two a day. Every time she talks on the phone to anyone, she says something like, "Well, I got my eighth mole today." And then whoever is on the other end must be right interested, because next she tells exactly how it happened. "I got him out near the corn." Then there's a pause, and she says, "Right before dinner."

I just roll my eyes about this without her seeing me, of course, because there is almost nothing Nana hates worse than eye rolling. Usually I'm in the other room, anyway, so there's no way she can see me making disrespectful faces about her mole killing. I have often wanted to ask my granddaddy what he thinks God thinks about Nana. Not so much Nana killing the moles, because I know that Granddaddy used to hunt, and he and I both fish a lot, too. But what, I wonder, does God think about Nana being so happy about killing moles every day? If it was me talking that way about something I did, I think that Nana would say I was being boastful. Not only that, but I kind of think God made the moles just like He made Nana. He can't be too thrilled about the idea of all His moles in northeast Mississippi hiding out in fear of being hoed to death by Nana.

While we fix lunch, we talk about the onions, the egg, the sweet milk, and the oil that go in with the cornmeal to make the hush puppies. We don't talk about custody. Nana tells me that Aunt Sarah always puts sugar in her hush puppies. I know her saying this is going to start a fuss.

Aunt Sarah, who is standing right there, says, "Lucy, make them however you usually do."

"Whatever you want to do, Sarah, is all right with me. I don't usually put sugar in hush puppies, but you can if you want to" is what Nana replies.

"Naw, that's all right. Make 'em your way," says Aunt Sarah. They go back and forth about this until Nana finally goes on and puts the sugar in the bowl.

Nana can't even eat hush puppies, because of her corn allergy. She has to roll her fish in flour instead of meal, too, which just isn't as good. She has to do her okra the same way, or she'll have a run-in with bronchitis. Nana has a list of about a million other things she can't eat, including shrimp, peaches, pepper, peanuts, crab, tomatoes, and even more. She talks about her allergies a lot, and I think all of us have them memorized, but she likes to remind everybody, anyway.

The FryDaddy, what we cook the fish in, is a dangerous appliance. Even Nana gets bad burns from oil popping out, almost every time we eat fish. I am old enough now to drop the fish and the hush puppies one by one into the fryer, but Nana still takes them out when they float to the top. I know that I could do that part, too, but she thinks I am going to burn my arm like she does. I just think she moves too fast; I am slower, more like my granddaddy.

We still don't talk about my daddy, or why I wanted to come home, or what custody is, and I hope that means everything really is all right. Nana seems happy that I'm next to her, and once, she even says so.

My job now is to watch everything cook and to tell Nana or Aunt Sarah when anything is ready to come out. It takes the fish longer than the hush puppies, and I always call them to pull it out too early, before it's golden brown like Nana says it ought to be. I just can't wait. I could eat fish every day, even if I had to catch, clean, and cook them all by myself.

Granddaddy Tate and I caught some of these fish this very day. Shoplifter Jim and his daddy, Big Jim, caught some, too. Big Jim uses real worms to catch fish, and this always makes me sad. It's not that I mind holding a worm or anything, but I just feel a little bit mean having to push the entire worm's body over the hook in order to trick the fish.

Granddaddy uses stinky Catfish Charlie to catch the fish. I have never said this to Nana or Granddaddy, but

Catfish Charlie reminds me of poop. It's brown and soft and smells worse than anything I've ever smelled. You use it the same as you would a worm; by that I mean the entire hook has to be covered up completely with it. The fish are good at telling if it's a trick. I always put extra Catfish Charlie on my hook so there is no question in the fish's mind about what is going on.

I am good at fishing because I have been doing it for so long. Granddaddy taught me everything about it. Even though he still takes the catch off the hook, most everything else I do by myself. Because catfish have long whiskers that can sting your hand, he will not let me take a fish off the hook yet. Even the baby ones, those that have to be thrown back in, he does himself. I watch how he uses his thumb and his pointer finger to hold the whiskers back and the other hand to jiggle the fish around until it comes off. Sometimes, even with Granddaddy doing it, the fish flips away and smacks him in the hand with a whisker. Granddaddy always says "Swannee!" when this happens. It cracks me up that he says "Swannee." He says "Swannee" where somebody like my daddy would probably say "Goddammit."

I love fishing with my granddaddy because he is so good, and plus he smiles at me in the kindest way. He uses his whole face to smile at me—eyelashes, head, and mouth all at once. He especially does that at certain times, like when I am tired of fishing but stay still, anyway, or when I put my own Catfish Charlie on the hook without his help and without making a fuss about how bad it smells.

You always know that Granddaddy would never ever wish to do anything that would hurt another living soul. Sometimes I swear he almost cries when it comes time to skin the fish. When we bring them back up to the house to get ready, he always says a prayer and straightaway apologizes to the fish. He calls them each "buddy," as in "Sorry, buddy, to have to do this," and then he slams the rock on the fish's head. Usually after about two blows, the fish is dead. He says it will hurt the fish less to be put out of its misery than to stay alive while he pulls the skin off and cuts it open for cleaning. It is hard to watch because it just seems like the meaner thing to do to kill the fish by mashing its head. But really, when I think about it, Granddaddy's way is nicer than dragging it out for a long time. I guess I would rather die real fast like that than have someone pull every bit of my skin off before cutting open my stomach.

Catfish skin is not scaly like most fish—it's smooth and slimy. The way to clean a catfish is to peel it like an orange, then chop off its head and cut the body into four or five pieces, including the tail. Some people like the tail the best because it's the most crunchy part after you fry it. Granddaddy hates the killing and cleaning, but he loves the taste, just like me.

Granddaddy Tate doesn't do a lot of explaining or talking about things. You have to learn just by watching him. I do think it makes him feel better that I am there with him when he's killing the fish. After he knocks them out with the rock, he looks up at me each time and says, "I hate to do that." Then he takes the next fish off the line and does the same thing with the same rock.

I have to say, I'd choose a big fish fry over Thanksgiving turkey or Easter ham or even Christmas dinner. The fish is just so juicy and sweet; it's better than any dessert I have ever tasted. Today, I eat seven pieces of fish, but I don't take any slaw because that is just a waste of room in my stomach.

Big Jim, from the other end of the picnic table hollers, "Georgia Tate, you saving room for that watermelon you've been babying all day?" My granddaddy looks up to see what I'll say.

"Yes, sir," I say. Then I swipe one more tiny piece of fish, because as good as it is right now, it will not be this yummy as leftovers.

After we get done eating, I am too stuffed for watermelon, but I can't say this to Granddaddy Tate. Sometimes he is like a little child. He gets so excited about things that most people don't even think once about, like a cold watermelon. We've been talking about and taking care of the watermelon all day now. He's been asking me, too, if I'm ready for it. "I can hear that watermelon getting cold, can't you?" I just giggle when he says that; he always tries to make me laugh by saying goofy things.

Granddaddy spreads newspaper all along the picnic table and cracks the watermelon open with a big kitchen knife. Then he starts slicing off pieces for each kid and saves one big piece for himself. The other grownups eat lemon pie or watermelon that is warm from having not been in the bathtub all day. Granddaddy Tate uses almost half a shaker of salt on his piece. He keeps trying to pass me the salt. Over and over I tell him, "No, thank you, I don't like salt on mine." He seems surprised by that, but I never have liked salt and watermelon together. Shoplifter Jim still gets a slice of cold watermelon even though he is in college now. In my mind, once someone starts college they ought to not be part of the kids' group anymore.

Jim is spitting watermelon seeds out with every bite. What is so disgusting is that Jim chews tobacco. So his mouth is filthy with tobacco juice all the time. When he spits out his watermelon seeds, they don't even land on

CHAPTER FIVE

Aunt Mazel is so lovely. Her skin is brown from the sun, and it makes her hair look white as a cloud. Unlike other really old ladies who have long hair, Aunt Mazel hardly ever wears hers up in a bun. Instead, it is long and flowing down her back. Now we are rocking in the porch swing and Aunt Mazel is singing "At Calvary," about Jesus dying for us on the cross. This is a different kind of singing, too. It's not like what happens to me sometimes—she isn't just singing this song because it's in her head and it has to get out. She is singing it right to me, right into my eyes while she holds my hand:

"*Mercy there was great and grace was free,*

Pardon there was multiplied to me.

There my burdened soul found liberty, at Calvary."

I don't really know what the words mean, but Aunt Mazel is singing them, and lightning bugs are firing up the whole yard just because she is singing, it seems. I start crying in the quiet and the dark. I am just so happy to be home, and happy that our country is doing fine after two hundred years, and I'm happy that I'm full of catfish.

Now I am crying so hard that I can't stop, and this makes Aunt Mazel smile big. She nods at me and she sings even louder. My shoulders are shaking and my nose is running bad. Aunt Mazel puts my head in her lap and uses the skirt of her dress to wipe my face off. This seems so wonderful of her. I didn't even want to look at the watermelon seeds that Jim spat from his mouth, but here is Aunt Mazel wiping my snot with her dress. I think she must love me. Then it's like she reads my mind, because as soon as I finish thinking that, she pushes my hair out of my face and whispers, "*Jesus* really loves you." She stops singing, and we swing on the porch without talking for a long time. Her thumbless hand is pushing my hair around and around my ear. Finally, I ask her, "Aunt Mazel? What happened to your thumb?"

"Hon, it got blowed off by a firecracker when I was five years old."

Right as she says that, Shoplifter Jim and his daddy, Big Jim, start lighting firecrackers. I expect Aunt Mazel to be a little bit scared, but she tells me to come on. And we go over to where they are, and we light firecrackers, too. Well, I only light a sparkler, but Aunt Mazel is lighting firecrackers and throwing them every bit as far as Jim and his daddy are throwing theirs. I am a little nervous that she might lose her other thumb. It's been ninety years since that last accident, and anything could happen. But Aunt Mazel is just laughing and having fun.

After the ten o'clock news is over, everybody starts to leave. We stand in the driveway forever, waving and hugging and kissing and trying to get everyone to take food with them. They won't even get home before midnight, but this happens every time. The first thing Aunt Sarah always says at the beginning of the day when they first pull up is, "Now, Lucy, we can't stay as late as we did last time. I'd like to be on the road by nine." Then my nana always says, "Now, listen, if it gets too late, just stay here. We've got plenty of room. The sofa bed pulls out, there is a double bed in Georgia Tate's room, and we can make pallets for the children. So don't worry about getting on the road at a certain time."

This is how it always goes, whether it's Fourth of July or Thanksgiving or Easter. And sooner or later Aunt Sarah puts an end to it all by saying, "Lucy, we're going home and that's that." Then Nana starts telling them to at least take some food with them. Finally, the only people left are Nana, Granddaddy Tate, Aunt Mazel, and me.

Aunt Mazel and I are sleeping together in the guest room tonight. She is dressed up for bed. In her long white nightgown she is even more lovely than usual. I hardly ever sleep in the guest room, but that's where we're sleeping. The sheets on this bed are way nicer than my sheets. We just put our regular sheets right on the bed from the dryer, but these sheets are cold and soft, and Nana even ironed them before she put them on the bed. These are white sheets, with narrow blue, pink, and yellow stripes like the colors of Easter eggs and Easter dresses. In my old T-shirt and panties, I am not dressed right to be sleeping in here.

All the girl cousins love to brush Aunt Mazel's hair. I would like to, also, but I don't want her to think that I only like her because of her pretty hair, so I don't even ask. She brushes her own hair while I count the strokes all the way up to two hundred, the same number as the bicentennial. She reads a psalm from the Bible and does something I have never heard before. She reads the words and puts my name in where God is supposed to be talking. She looks me right in my eyes and says, "Let Your face shine upon Your servant Georgia Tate and save her in Your kindness. Amen."

When Aunt Mazel says my name, I think how my mama would be saying it that way, too—soft and slow like there is no one else in the world with that name. Maybe there isn't. I wish that Aunt Mazel would stay with us forever. I fall asleep while she has the light on and is reading the Bible to herself.

In the night, I dream that I am walking barefoot up a great hill. My feet are bleeding, but I am going to make it to the big white cross at the top. I am alone and wearing a white cotton nightgown, just like Aunt Mazel's. When I reach the top, the sky gets dark black and the wind starts to blow the treetops like crazy. Birds are fussing and there is nowhere for me to get out of the storm. I am scared and alone.

I must be crying hard in my sleep, because when I wake up, Granddaddy Tate and Nana are both standing over top of me, looking worried. Aunt Mazel is sitting straight up in bed, and she is the one who asks why I am crying. When I tell them my dream, Aunt Mazel hands her Bible to my granddaddy and he asks me to pray with him. Nana's lips get tight like they always do in church, and she closes her eyes even tighter and bows her head.

I think how funny Granddaddy Tate looks holding a Bible in his undershorts and undershirt. I have never seen him undressed like this. Even when he is in church with his black robe on, I know for a fact he wears a whole suit underneath. I wonder if he feels funny in front of God, holding the Bible, almost naked and all. His boxers are light blue with little checks, and he wears a real scoop-necked undershirt, not a T-shirt. He still has his black socks on, and I keep thinking about whether Granddaddy Tate pulled his socks on specially to come in here, or if he sleeps in them.

The three of them are praying now. Granddaddy Tate has his hand on my head, and Nana and Aunt Mazel are bowed real low and all. Then Granddaddy says, "Georgia Tate, are you ready to make a decision for Christ?" I look at him for what must be too long, because Aunt Mazel and Nana snap their heads up and they seem to be waiting for something special from me. The truth is that I don't know what kind of decision for Christ Granddaddy Tate wants me to make. I am wondering if it is to pick up Jim-the-shoplifter's disgusting watermelon seeds that will be baked into the patio and picnic table by lunchtime tomorrow. It seems like this must be it, and I am willing to pick those seeds up after all, for Jesus. So I nod yes. Now his hands are on my head again and Nana and Aunt Mazel are crying and they are all happy. We are all hugging there in the guest room.

CHAPTER SIX

Early the next morning, Granddaddy Tate and I go into town to get the mail, like always. Nana and Aunt Mazel stay at home and work in the garden. They get along real well together, even though Aunt Mazel is Granddaddy's aunt, not Nana's.

Aunt Mazel is the only family Granddaddy has left besides Nana and me. He is always trying to talk her into living with us, but she won't do it. Nana says she and Aunt Mazel are enough alike that it would be easy to have her around. We have plenty of room in the house, too. But Aunt Mazel says she is too old to change what she's been doing for so long. She just laughs whenever Granddaddy brings up the subject.

Granddaddy drives his big truck, and I feel happy riding beside him. There is a nice smell in the truck. Granddaddy never wears cologne, not even to church. So the truck smell is the smell of his skin. It's not a bad smell, and normally you have to get real close to him, like when you're giving him a hug or something, to smell it. But the whole truck is just full of it. I don't know how to describe it, but I reckon it smells like a combination of the garden, fishing, and a little hard work. It's what I would call the smell of outside once it gets onto you. I like it.

On the seat of the truck, there is a wild-turkey leg that has been here ever since I can remember. It's not a drumstick, like you would eat at Thanksgiving. It's a skinny, wrinkly leg and claw. On turkey legs in the grocery store, this part is already off. The only way you get this kind of turkey leg is to cut it off the turkey yourself. The picture in my mind of him killing a turkey doesn't fit with Granddaddy Tate, who is the most gentle person I ever met. One time I asked him where he got it. He acted almost embarrassed, then said, "I shot that turkey." I wanted to ask if he ate the turkey later, but he seemed to not want to talk about it. I did ask him, "Why did you cut the leg off, and why do you keep it in the truck?"

"To remind me how hard it was to finally get a turkey" is what he said.

We're driving around the square and I am thinking about all these things when Granddaddy says, "Georgia Tate, today is a special day. You belong to Christ now, so you need your own Bible." I am happy about this and hope that I can talk Nana into getting me my own nightgown like Aunt Mazel's to go with it. When we pull into the newspaper office, where they sell all kinds of Bibles, Granddaddy lets me pick out whichever one I want. There are all different kinds of Bibles. There is one for children, called the *Living Bible,* with a picture of Jesus holding a lamb, and then a pretty white one with golden letters on the front. I like them both very much.

I think of Granddaddy's Bible that he uses to prepare his sermons and how old it must be. The leather is cracked and some of the pages are torn. He has read it so much that it's soft and bendy in his hands. I decide to get the white one, which is just like his, except Granddaddy's is black, and we order my name, Georgia Tate Jamison, to be printed on the bottom right corner in the same golden letters that say HOLY BIBLE, only smaller.

On the inside, the white one has the same picture of Jesus with the lamb that's on the outside of the *Living Bible,* so I feel like I'm getting sort of a two-for-one deal.

While we're waiting for them to put my name on the cover, Granddaddy and I drive around the square, doing errands. We stop by City Drug to pick up Nana's prescription, we get the mail, and Granddaddy makes me sit in the truck while he runs into McCann's Funeral Home. I know why he stopped; the Presbyterians all use McCann's. And today the hearse is here, and it's pulled up to the side door. Somebody has died. I don't know who it is; Granddaddy doesn't seem to know, either, because he acted surprised when he saw the hearse. Usually, he and Nana are the first ones to know who has died, and how, and where everything will take place. I have never seen a dead body before. I think seeing one would scare me and make it hard to go to sleep at night, especially if I saw the dead body of someone that I love, and they just looked asleep, like Nana says they do.

I don't remember my mama or seeing her body; I only remember her being gone. For as far back as I can stretch my mind, I don't remember her. I have heard that I was with her when she died. Nana says she was real sick for a long time. I think she had pneumonia and just died with it. I know how pretty she was, because I have pictures of her that I pull out and look at. She looks some like me, but mostly people say I look like my daddy.

It is getting too hot sitting in the truck, and I can

hardly breathe, even when I put the windows down. Granddaddy must know the body inside, because he is taking so long. I hop out and climb into the truck bed and lie down in the back. That way I am officially still in the truck. The clouds are big, beautiful cumulus clouds. We learned about cumulus clouds in science last year. I got straight A's, but I have to say that studying about clouds and the weather was my favorite lesson of everything we learned. I even won second place with my science project about clouds. I made a cloud in a glass box, and Granddaddy helped me.

I could lie here looking at clouds all day long and never be bored. When I am outside, it's easier to be me. I can get on my bike and ride around all day—from our house, into town—and never run into one single wall. Not much can break outside, either, and if I spill something, who cares? Nobody cares outside, not even Nana.

Reading is another place where there aren't any walls, and I can go even farther away with a book than I can get on my bike. Nana says that I am a very advanced reader like my mama, who was the best in her class all through high school and graduated right before I was born. They didn't let her be valedictorian, because she had missed so many classes from morning sickness and going to the doctor and all. It was more than just grades that counted; it was also attendance. So even though she had the very highest grades, she didn't get to be first in her class. Nana is still a little mad about that.

When my granddaddy comes out, I ask him, "Who was it?" That is exactly how I've heard Nana ask the question on other days. He tells me that the body in McCann's is a boy named Tommy Bragg, from our church. He was in a car wreck last night on Highway 4. His daddy is our doctor, and his mama is the librarian, not at school but at the city library. Lots of people are going to be real sad. Tommy Bragg was always winning something for Tippah County—a basketball game, a football game, a swim meet. He was supposed to go to Ole Miss to play basketball this coming year. My daddy was like that, too. He was always winning something for Tippah County. I know that from looking at my mama's old high school yearbooks; they were in the same grade. He wasn't as smart as my mama, but he was a really accomplished athlete. They look like opposites in the yearbooks. She was president of the Latin Club and the Science Club and the student government, and he was captain of all of the teams.

CHAPTER SEVEN

Revival starts tonight, and there are two preachers: my granddaddy and a guest preacher from Little Rock. Tonight, Granddaddy is preaching a sermon called "The Glory of God." If you ask me, the whippoorwill we heard singing at the pond caused him to change it to that from "Brothers in Christ." We had been fishing, and I asked him, "Why are you only calling it 'Brothers in Christ' and not 'Brothers and Sisters in Christ'?"

He said, "Because the twelve disciples were like brothers to Jesus."

"Granddaddy, don't you think Mary Magdalene and Martha must have been like his sisters? They seem to have been around him all of the time."

"Probably, but they weren't in the twelve. Only the twelve were with Jesus at the Last Supper."

I hated to do it, because Granddaddy knows way more about the Bible and Jesus than I do. But I remembered the story of the lady who poured perfume all over Jesus, and she did that at the Last Supper; I know, because Judas got all mad about it. When I told Granddaddy that, I tried hard to do it in a nice way, not in a smarty-pants way. He looked like he was going to say something, but then my cork went under and he had to help me reel in my fish. We ended up throwing it back because it was a brim, which are too bony to eat. The fish seemed to have made him forget about the "Brothers in Christ" sermon. But just then, we heard a whippoorwill singing, and Granddaddy said, "The glory of God is all around us," and that became his sermon.

Revival starts every night at six o'clock and goes on until about eight. In addition to the two preachers, there is extra music and an altar call during the service. Every night there is a supper right after. On the last night, homecoming night, everyone brings something, and double or triple the number of people show up.

During the first few nights, the women's circle rotates

who prepares the meal. Tonight's supper is ham, potato salad, three-bean salad (which I can't stand), sliced tomatoes, corn on the cob, rolls, and peach cobbler. The ladies who serve the meal don't come to the service because they're busy fixing up everything.

The rest of us stay inside church and try to get saved. I have already been saved—more than once, if you ask me. When I was a baby, my granddaddy baptized me; to me, that counts as officially being saved. Then, on the Fourth of July, according to Nana, Granddaddy Tate, and Aunt Mazel, I made a decision for Christ. I guess the way it works is that the grownups make the decision for you when you're a baby. When you grow up a little, you decide it again for yourself.

Almost everybody here tonight has probably been baptized and made a decision for Christ already. Sometimes there are new people or people who have let their decision for Christ get watered down a little. The purpose of revival—with the special food and special preaching—is to bring some life back into everybody's promise to God and to bring some life back into the church.

The special music tonight is Suzie Settlemeyer, who is only seven years old. She is singing two songs, "Precious Lord" and "Somebody's Knocking." Every revival, Suzie, her daddy, and her mama get up at least one night and sing. She must have been only four years old the first time. Her daddy plays the bass guitar and sings in the background, and her mama plays the piano. When Suzie opens her mouth to sing, it doesn't even sound like a child's voice. She doesn't even look like a child when she's singing.

I love to sing, and I can even carry a tune. I don't know that I could ever sing like Suzie does. It's something more than just her voice that's booming and showy. It's like her whole little body fills with the Grand Ole Opry and then just lets loose.

The guest preacher is young and what I would call fancy—too fancy for New Life Presbyterian Church, in my opinion. He is wearing a khaki suit and a bow tie. He's not even wearing a robe. My granddaddy always wears his black robe and a stole. Tonight Granddaddy is wearing a red, white, and blue stole that one of the old ladies from the church made him. I think it's supposed to look like the flag for Independence Day.

It's hard for me to pay attention to the Little Rock preacher because I am pretty tightly packed in between Nana and Aunt Mazel. They are both wearing dresses without sleeves, and they are both sweating pretty good. It's real hot in here, and this little church doesn't have even one air conditioner. All of the windows are open, so every now and then a breeze blows through, and it feels so good I could cry. I can tell from here that Aunt Mazel doesn't shave her underarms, because little gray hairs are peeking out. She doesn't shave her legs, either; I always knew about her legs, but not about her underarms. She is wearing her long hair up in a twisted bun tonight.

What the Little Rock preacher is saying is that he was in Israel last year, walking the exact steps Jesus walked. The point of this is that Jesus suffered a lot—which we all knew already. Then the preacher says that while he was in Israel, he made up his own crown of thorns and pushed it down over his own head, until his forehead began to bleed. He says, "I could bear the pain no more, but I pressed on, to feel pain that Jesus felt."

I figure he is making this up. He is outright lying to us. But he is really on a roll, and people are listening. He starts saying that our suffering is nothing compared to the suffering of Jesus. That was the whole point of his putting on the crown of thorns—that he couldn't take even a sample of the pain that Jesus felt.

I don't believe Jesus would say that our suffering is nothing compared to his own. I'm thinking that Tommy Bragg's parents would gladly wear that crown of thorns every day if they could get that boy back. To my way of thinking, this preacher has got it backward. If Jesus were at the pulpit, he would be saying, "I know that you suffer. I lived on this earth, too, and I know for a fact that it's hard and painful sometimes." I think Jesus would preach more of a message of understanding. This one from Little Rock is just about telling people their hurts don't amount to much.

When Suzie Settlemeyer starts singing "Somebody's Knocking," the preacher calls for people to come down to the altar. About six people go: four teenagers, who you know just go because they want to be together, and two men. That's not too bad. But my granddaddy has got as many as thirty to the altar before, and not by telling them that their hurting doesn't count.

After the service, we all go outside to eat. There are picnic tables under the covered shelter, and two long tables with the food laid out. The Little Rock preacher goes through the line first because he is our guest. People aren't paying much attention to anything, and all of the children—except me—are running wild. I don't know any of these kids real well, and they're mostly younger. There is one boy who is in my grade, and we already said hello. Plus, being Granddaddy and Nana's means I can't run around getting into trouble.

The four teenagers—two boys and two girls—who went to the altar are now smoking cigarettes and hanging all over each other in the parking lot. Suzie Settlemeyer is showing anybody who will look all of the mosquito bites she has all over her body. Nobody really knows what to do when she opens her drawers to show that she even has one on her privates. Suzie doesn't mind at all; she is sitting right on the porch steps, legs wide open, and peeling back her panties, saying, "Look here. I got a big one right on my tee-tee." Then, I swear, she reaches down and scratches the big bite on her "tee-tee," in front of the whole world. I make myself a reminder to watch where those hands go next and to stay out of the potato chip bowl, where I know Suzie already has been.

Until revival started, most nights since July Fourth, Aunt Mazel, Granddaddy, Nana, and I would all four play Scrabble or Rook together and eat ice cream. The three of them like homemade ice cream. I myself would rather have ice milk, all stirred up with chocolate syrup until it is soft like the Tastee-Freez. Nana, Granddaddy, and Aunt Mazel eat their ice cream with angel food cake and strawberries. That's good, but not as good as the way I like it.

We can play Scrabble anytime, even if it's just me and Nana playing while Granddaddy writes a sermon. But when Aunt Mazel is here, we're more likely to play Rook because we have a fourth person and we can play teams.

It's like we're all on vacation. I get to stay up late, Nana doesn't worry about chores so much, and there's more laughing and joking around. Tomorrow we'll drive Aunt Mazel home to Moulton. I will really miss her.

CHAPTER EIGHT

My mama never got to rub her hands on my hair like Aunt Mazel does. She never got to sit next to me at breakfast all snuggly like Nana does. According to Nana, Mama was sick for a while after I was born and she never got better, so she died. Nana says my mama is in heaven. She says my mama only knows me from there, and from me being in her womb.

Today Ginger and I went swimming at Tippah Lake, and she told me the truth. I mean, the real truth. I know she wasn't planning on it. Seems like nobody was ever planning on telling me.

This was the first time all summer we'd been out to Tippah Lake. Last summer, we'd go every week, sometimes every day. Ginger prefers Tippah Lake because it's not as crowded as the city pool. I prefer the pool because it's cleaner. Except for the bugs that die in the chlorine, the city pool is definitely cleaner.

Nobody seems to care as much about keeping the lake clean. There's always cigarette butts, candy wrappers, and hair floating around in the water. They made the lake with white sand all around it, like a pretend beach so you feel like you're at the ocean. If you forget about the lake being man-made, and if you don't look at it too closely, it's as beautiful as a postcard lake tucked away in the mountains, only without the mountains. But in some places the water is still just disgusting.

Nana and Mrs. Parsons had dropped us off to spend the whole day together. Ginger and me, we swim a lot, and we don't give the lifeguard any trouble. I usually bring a lunch that Nana packs for me. Ginger eats her lunch from the candy machine—a PayDay bar, Nabs, and a Coke.

Anyway, today me and Ginger got into a fight. She thinks I think I know everything. I tried to tell her that I know I don't know everything, but that when I do speak up, I am right. Normally I don't say anything if I think I might be wrong.

She said, "See, that's what I mean. You think you know everything. You think you know more than me, but you don't—not about everything. There's some things I know that you aren't even close to knowing."

All I said was, "Okay." But she could probably tell that I didn't mean "Okay, you're right." What I really meant was "Okay, if that's what you think." Because the truth is, in most ways, I am pretty much smarter than Ginger. I'm not as brave or even as curious as she is, but she knows me pretty well and she's right: I do think I know more than she does.

"You don't even know the truth about your own mama," she said real loud, almost yelling at me.

"Yes, I do."

"Okay, tell me."

"Why? You know it, too. She died when I was a brand-new baby. She was real sick and she died." All of a sudden I could hear myself saying it like I wasn't so sure myself anymore.

"Everybody in the whole town knows except you. Everybody knows she tried to shoot herself in the heart."

I just stood there, looking at her, half wondering, Do I really want to know this? and half thinking, Ginger is a liar and I should sock her in the face. Ginger was looking at the sand and pushing it around with her red-painted toenails. She already looked like she was wishing she could take it all back real quick. I was getting ready to call her a liar, when I saw that her face had turned pale like she had got too much sun with not enough to drink. Right then I knew she was telling the truth.

"I'm sorry, Georgia Tate. I sure am sorry."

"Tell me the whole thing," I said.

"That's all I know, Georgia Tate; you were a tiny baby, and your mama tried to shoot herself with your granddaddy's hunting gun."

"Where did she do it?"

I could see that Ginger was scared and didn't want to get in trouble. Even Ginger's mama, who Nana says is on the prowl and doesn't care much about being a good mother, would've smacked Ginger on the face for telling me something like this. But Ginger is my best friend. It's one of those things friends do without really talking about it. So I knew I needed to ask all the questions and let Ginger pretend that I made her tell me. This was all okay with me, so I asked her again, "Where did she do it?"

"Green-Old-Field. She left the car running, too." Green-Old-Field is off Highway 15, across from First Monday—the biggest market in the mid-South. The field is tucked in below the railroad tracks and the highway, so when it rains, the field floods and holds water too long to plant cotton or soybeans. Green-Old-Field lies fallow every year.

"Where was I?" She didn't answer, even after I asked her a couple more times. "Do you want me to be mad at you forever? Just tell me, where was I?"

"Well, you were in the car, too."

I don't like it when people yell at me, and I know Ginger doesn't, either. Sometimes, though, it's the hollering that gets results. Somewhere inside, we both knew we weren't really mad at each other, but I needed the full story. So I yelled a little bit: "I knew you knew more. How could you know that I was in the car, too, and not even plan on telling me? We're talking about my mama, and we are talking about me, Ginger Parsons. If you know about this, you have to tell me in order to stay friends."

I knew that Ginger was going to tell me, and Ginger knew that I wasn't going to stop being her friend.

"That's really all I know except that Dr. Bragg recognized your mama's car from the road, and he found y'all. You were screaming and crying, probably because you were hungry."

"No, probably because guns are loud, and I wanted my mama."

Ginger has never been a tender type of person. But she reached her hand up and pushed my hair out of my eyes as if she were all grown up. She said, "Georgia Tate, I wish I had told you before. I kept thinking that one of these days your nana would tell you."

I brushed her hand off of me, then said, "You said she *tried* to shoot herself in the heart."

"She ain't dead, Georgia Tate."

The way she said it, like I was dumb or something for not figuring it out, made me mad as heck.

"Nana says she's dead. She died with pneumonia."

"You ever visit her grave?" Ginger asked me.

"No." It was the truth, and I had never even thought about asking to visit Mama's grave.

"You ever even seen her grave or heard anybody talk about going to put flowers on it at Christmas or Easter?"

"No."

"Well, if she was dead, that ain't right, is it? To not visit somebody's grave at Christmas and Easter, or maybe their birthday—that ain't right. We visit the graves of people I don't even know, and you don't even visit the grave of your own mama? Maybe there ain't no grave."

I didn't say one word. It was my turn to push the sand around with my toenails, only my toenails are not painted red. They're not painted at all.

Then she asked me, "What does your granddaddy say about your mama?"

"Not much. Sometimes he says I'm like her. Sometimes, if I ask, he says he misses her. I asked him once if he thought she was in heaven, and he said he didn't know."

"See?"

"See what?"

"See, she ain't dead, Georgia Tate."

But I just kept quiet. She didn't say anything else.

"Well?" I said.

"Well, what?"

"Well, where is she?" This time I said it like Ginger was the dumb one, mainly so she could have a taste of her own attitude.

"I don't know anything for sure. It's just what I've heard. She tried to shoot herself dead, then she just wasn't right after that. But I think she got sent to East Mississippi State Hospital, in Meridian. The insane asylum." That last part was Ginger trying to be Miss Know-It-All.

"Do you even know what 'insane asylum' means?" I was being real smart right back at her now.

"It's where they send crazy people. The crazy teenagers especially all go to East Mississippi State."

I figured Ginger was probably right about where she was sent. Even though my mama would not be a teenager anymore, she was only seventeen when she died. Or when she didn't die.

"Do you think she was crazy?" I asked Ginger, and I hoped that she could see and hear that the right answer was No, your mama is not crazy. But she did not answer.

"Do you think she was crazy?" I asked again, and I held my breath for Ginger's answer.

Poor old Ginger was holding her breath hard, too, because her answer came pouring out of her like it had been holed up in there for a good long time. "I think she probably isn't crazy. She was probably hurting an awful lot inside and feeling kind of alone. You don't know what it's like to live in this town if you make a mistake or if you're different. Your mama knew, and I do, too. You think I don't know what even your nana thinks about me and my mama? Because we're poor? Because my daddy left? You got it pretty easy around here, Georgia Tate. Everybody around here tries to protect you from how you're different on account of your mama getting pregnant, then shooting herself, and on account of your granddaddy being a big preacher. So no, I don't think she was crazy; I just think it might all have been too much for one girl to carry."

I didn't say one word. I wanted to say everything all at once, but I didn't know which thing was the right thing to say. I wanted to say it's not fair, and I wanted to say I hated Ginger for not telling me before now. But all that would've been a lie. I half wanted to ask Ginger to run away with me to find my mama, but the truth is, that would be too scary. The worst part was that I didn't even feel happy at the thought of my mama not being dead. Her being alive or, I guess, my knowing about her being alive changed everything. Knowing about her being alive

CHAPTER NINE

Nana and I are eating honey buns for breakfast. There is no sound in the house except for the two of us sitting quietly in the kitchen and the clock in the living room. Sometimes I like to sleep late on Saturdays, but when I heard the clock strike seven, I knew Nana would be in the kitchen. These mornings, with just the two of us, are my favorite. Today, she pours me coffee. I have tasted Nana's coffee before—it's so sweet, with lots of milk and sugar. I want my coffee to taste just like hers. Granddaddy will be up in an hour or so, and then we will go to town to visit and get the mail.

I am relieved to be here with Nana, and I want everything to be the same as it was before—the way it was even before I went to Jacksonville. More than anything, I want to sit right inside Nana's arm and lean my head on her shoulder and feel how soft her body is and how safe it is inside her arms. But we're not even sitting next to each other; we're facing each other—only I can't see much of Nana's face because she won't look at me.

When she picked me up from Tippah Lake yesterday, what Ginger told me about my mama came flooding out before I had time to block it. Every bit of color, even the color from Nana's lipstick, drained from her face in about three seconds flat. I was kicking myself that I hadn't waited until we got home or until after supper. But the words just came tumbling out. "I know about my mama. I mean, the truth."

"Your mama died, Georgia Tate. That is the truth."

As much as I had wished it to be so, I knew Nana was lying to me. I thought she probably had good reasons to lie, but it seemed like we ought to start talking about what is real and what's not, now that I finally knew. For the rest of the ride home and the rest of the evening, Nana didn't say a word to me at all. Not one word.

Right now, I am watching her while I eat my breakfast, and I wish she would just talk. This will not be a normal breakfast, where she is warm and squishy, and I can tuck myself into her arms while we plan our day or talk about anything. This morning Nana is straight and hard as a board, and I can already see that she is not about to bend one inch.

I am needing Nana to talk to me, to tell me that nothing has really changed. I want her to tell me that I will never have to go to Jacksonville again, and that she and Granddaddy and I are a family and our belonging together will never change—not on account of my mama or my daddy; not even on account of me, or of anything I could ever do; and not on account of custody.

"I know about my mama. I mean the truth," I say, like I did in the car yesterday. Nana's back slumps and her pink face again turns something less than white.

"Well, I doubt if you know the truth. You might think you do. We're not going to talk about that right now." She says this as though I had broken a lamp or something.

Usually, I would just say, "Yes, ma'am," or something respectful like that. But today I do something I have never, ever done.

"Yes, we are. You've been lying about her for my whole life." Nana doesn't say a word, but she looks like she is going to explode. I keep on talking. "She ain't dead." I say these words exactly how Ginger said them to me. I never say "ain't." But this time it sounds right, because if nothing else will get her talking to me, then saying "ain't" will. "Why did you lie about it?" I add, trying to make her say something.

"Georgia Tate, are you calling me a liar?"

"Yes, ma'am."

She is looking at me full in the face now, and I am looking at her. I don't want her to explode, because I know I won't be able to fix her. But there is nothing I can do. I feel like I will never have Nana back with me again, like now she is against me.

In a way, ever since my trip to Jacksonville, I actually feel older than Nana. I know more about the world than she does. She knows Granddaddy, and she knows this town. She's never been anywhere but around here. No matter where you go within a few hundred miles, it's all the same thing. Whether it's Selma or Florence or Tupelo—it's all about the same. She knows our kitchen and the garden and her women's circle. But she doesn't know about people being so angry that they punch each other, or people saying "goddammit" with every other word. She doesn't know about being so ashamed that your mind takes you to a faraway, made-up place. All of those are the things, I think, that make her so angry with me. When she looks at me, she can see everything she doesn't know, and she doesn't want me to know it, either.

"Georgia, go on back to your room. Spend the rest of the day there, while I decide what we're going to do about your attitude."

"Okay," I say. "I love you, Nana." She doesn't even say it back.

"I said, 'I love you, Nana.'"

I throw my arms around her neck and hold tight to her because I want her to say it, too, and I want her to tell me that everything will be all right. And most of all, I want her to call me sweet child, but she doesn't. She pats my shoulder and tells me, "Go on."

Here in my room is where I want to stay forever. I am lucky to have a double bed. Ginger Parsons does not have a double bed. She doesn't even have her own room. Ginger has to share a room with her two little sisters, even though her younger brother gets his own room. On a double bed, there is room to stretch way out and think, and there is room to look out the window at the sky and the trees. My white Bible and my alarm clock are beside the bed, just like they always are, every day. According to my nightstand, everything is the same as it was before. But according to my insides, everything is different.

I hear the lawn mower. When Nana finishes cutting the grass, I'll ask if I can come out of my room. Maybe she'll be ready to make up by then.

CHAPTER TEN

The clock wakes me up; I hear it chime three times. I know without having to look around that Granddaddy has gone to town without me. Nana has finished the grass, because there is no lawn mower sound. There is nothing coming from anywhere: no sounds besides the clock, no smells of dinner rolls or chicken casserole, no creaks in the floor to tell me if Nana is ironing or getting dinner ready.

My very first memory ever in my whole life is waking up from a nap when I was a little girl and not finding Nana. I don't know how old I was, old enough to be sleeping in a real bed—maybe three or four. I remember waking up to a quiet house, except for the clock ticking. I know the clock was ticking, because I can hear it in my mind when I think back. There were birds singing outside, but there was nothing else. I looked in every room in the house: the kitchen, the living room, the guest bedroom, Nana's room, and the laundry room. Then I went outside and looked everywhere, and there was no Nana. I cried and cried, standing there in the garden with this little blue pillow that I used to carry around with me. Finally, Nana came out there and scooped me up. She had been putting things away in the attic.

Today when I get up and go to the kitchen, I see a glass of tea on the counter, but Nana is on the floor. The sun is pouring in the window right onto her face, and she is lying on her side, asleep. The bottoms of her shoes still have blades of grass on them, and she doesn't answer me when I call. I bend low beside her ear and whisper, "Nana, Nana wake up." I kiss her on the ear. I shake her shoulders and nothing happens.

The woman who answers the phone at the hospital doesn't know where Booneville Road is, and she doesn't know who I am talking about when I say Brother Tate. This is the dumbest thing ever, because anyone who has been here for any length of time knows Granddaddy. Plus, there are only four white churches in town, if you count

Church of Christ, and we all know each other pretty good, anyway. This lady is not helping, and she doesn't believe that we don't have a street address. But we don't. We live on Booneville Road, and we have a box at the post office. Everyone but this lady knows where we live. I tell her that Nana is lying on the floor asleep but I can't wake her up. I describe everything about our house, about Granddaddy, about what's wrong with Nana. She says she still can't help me unless I give her a street address.

So I give her directions.

"Here's how you get here: take Highway 15 like you're going to New Albany, then turn left on Highway 4 like you're going to Iuka. Then turn right on Booneville Road, it's before you get to the country club, and—"

"I need a street address," she interrupts, and Nana is still on the floor.

"Don't you have any Presbyterians working there?" I say, in the most smart-mouth way I can.

"I'm sure we do, but that won't do your grandmother any good. I need a street address."

"Go find a Presbyterian. Tell them to drive the ambulance to Brother Tate's house. If you can't find a Presbyterian, find a Baptist or a Methodist. Anybody who goes to church every Sunday will know where I live."

"Fine, I'll dispatch an ambulance to Brother Tate's house."

She takes my name. I wait with Nana, beside her, until almost four o'clock. The ambulance pulls up and Granddaddy's truck is right behind it. The driver had asked Granddaddy, at the gas station, how to get to Brother Tate the Presbyterian preacher's house. He had been driving up and down Highway 4, looking for our house.

The rescue people decide to take Nana to Tupelo, instead of our hospital in town. They have more doctors and better stuff in Tupelo, so they can do more to help people who are in a bad way. Granddaddy and I follow the ambulance to Tupelo, but I know already that even Tupelo won't be good enough for Nana.

On the ride home, Granddaddy Tate doesn't speak. It seems as if he is hardly driving us. He's clinging to the steering wheel more like he is holding on than driving.

"Granddaddy, do you want me to drive?" He has let me drive the truck before, on our road and in our driveway, so I feel sure that I could drive now, on this road.

He shakes his head no and begins to cry. I am not crying. I am staring out the window, pretending that I live in every house we pass. I pretend to live alone with Granddaddy and wonder what we will do and how things will change without Nana. I wonder if Granddaddy knows how angry Nana was with me this morning. And I can't help wondering if he knows everything about what it was like in Florida.

"Granddaddy? Nana and I have been fussing a lot last night and today. This morning, she wouldn't say she loved me back."

He wipes his eyes and nods like he knows everything about it. "She could be like that. I bet right now she's wishing that she had said it first." That makes him cry even more. A part of me feels like I should leave him be to cry and feel sad. A bigger part of me needs to know if I made Nana so mad that her heart stopped.

"Did she tell you what we were fussing about?"

"She did. We talked about it for a long time last night after you were asleep. Nana and I thought the three of us should talk about it together. We were planning on taking you to Satterwhite's for dinner tonight and then going for a drive."

We usually go to Satterwhite's Fish House only on special occasions. It's my favorite restaurant ever. Satterwhite's is way out in the country, so it's a long drive just to get there and back. They only serve on Thursday, Friday, and Saturday, so you have to make advance reservations in order for them to know how much fish to fry.

At Satterwhite's, which really isn't much more than a big garage with four rows of picnic tables, they use plastic tablecloths of all different designs. Nana never used plastic tablecloths, but she commented that it was the only practical thing to do at Satterwhite's. There's no menu and no waitresses like there are in town at Sister's Diner. You just walk in, fix your plate and drink, and sit down and start eating. At the front of the restaurant is the cash register and a buffet table with fried catfish, fried chicken, fried okra, French fries, hush puppies, green beans, corn on the cob, and rolls. It's all you can eat, and I usually eat a lot.

The Satterwhites go to one of my granddaddy's country churches, New Covenant, so they are always real happy to see us come in. They even know to fix Nana's fish and okra with flour instead of cornmeal. I wonder if they fixed Nana's fish, thinking we would be there tonight. Probably they did. They probably wonder where we are, too.

"What were y'all planning on telling me?" I finally ask.

"We were going to tell you everything we know about your mama and what happened when you were a baby."

"Oh." That's all I say because that is all I need to hear to know that Ginger was right.

Granddaddy keeps on talking; he doesn't need me to say anything else. For now, he has stopped crying, and it's like he has been waiting for this day so he can finally relieve himself of this story. He tells me that it's true that my mama shot herself, tried to kill herself. It's true that I was in the car with her and that Dr. Bragg found us. Granddaddy tells it just the way Ginger did. He says Dr. Bragg recognized the car, and when he pulled up, he found Mama bleeding and unconscious, and me lying in the front seat with a diaper and a little T-shirt on, crying with all of my lungs.

She had shot herself more in her armpit than in her heart and was hurt bad enough to stay in the hospital for a while. Everybody expected her to come home and get better. But even though her body was going to get better, Dr. Bragg didn't think her mind would get better without some help. He said East Mississippi State Hospital would be a good place; troubled teenagers were their specialty. Granddaddy tells me that when Mama got sent to the insane asylum, that's when my daddy left.

"When she turned eighteen, they discharged her. She came home to tell us that she wasn't coming home. She said she needed to get some things straight. For a while, I thought she would come back in a few days, then a few weeks, then a few months. I gave up. We both gave up after a while. By the time you were old enough to ask questions and understand things, it had been several years since we'd heard from her. To us, especially to Nana, it's as if she did die. I guess that's why it didn't seem like a lie to Nana. To her, your mama did die."

Granddaddy reaches in his shirt pocket and hands me

an envelope that says only *Georgia Tate* on the outside. "Here," he says, "I planned on giving you this tonight."

I know without looking, it's from my mama. It has never been opened, so nobody, not even Granddaddy knows what it says. I know I don't have to, but I read it aloud for me and Granddaddy to hear together.

"Dear Georgia Tate,

You and I played together for a little bit today. That was real nice. You are the daughter that I have always dreamed of having for my own. I only wish I was ready.

If you are reading this letter, then I know you are having a lot of different feelings—about me, about Mama and Daddy, maybe even about your own life up to now. One thing I have learned about feelings is that they can only hurt you if you let them. There is so much that I'd like to share with you. The truth is that I am not ready to be anybody's mama. I need to learn to take care of myself and love myself before I can take care of and love you like you deserve.

I love you dearly and I will never be far away from you.

Love always,

Your mama"

Granddaddy starts crying again while I read this. His tears aren't loud like mine. His are the silent ones that run down your face with enough splash to start a big wet spot on your pants. I realize now that, even in the past, there was sometimes just sort of a sorrow—just in the way Granddaddy would say nothing. Just in the way he moves, even. And I wonder if that sorrow is about his still wanting to be my mama's daddy but not being able to.

"Granddaddy, do you think Nana got so mad at me that it killed her?"

"No, Georgia Tate. I think she was a stubborn old woman who mowed the lawn every Saturday, even Saturdays in July when anybody with any sense would have let it go until the day cooled off."

"Do you think if we had had a street address that she would not have died?"

"No, dolly, your nana was already gone when you found her. There is nothing about this that is your fault. God just wanted her home, with Him." Granddaddy is so tender when he says this that I believe him, because I know he is not just making it up for me to feel better.

I curl up with my Bible and fall asleep remembering Aunt Mazel and how happy I felt last week. I wonder if Nana is already in heaven. And I wonder if being in heaven means you can see and hear everything that anyone on Earth does or says or thinks. I hope this is not what happens. I would like some privacy from Nana, even though she must can understand things better now that she is with God. He probably explained everything to her in a way so she knows that I am not bad; I'm just me.

CHAPTER ELEVEN

Nana's funeral is packed with people; I have never seen some of them before. On the front row are Aunt Mazel, Granddaddy, me, and Aunt Sarah and her husband, Willard. Nana's brother and nephew—Big Jim and Shoplifter Jim—are pallbearers, along with some of the men from church. According to Aunt Sarah, Aunt Mazel should not be on the front row with us, because she is my Granddaddy's family, not Nana's. Aunt Mazel is not really even my aunt; she is my great-great-aunt. She is the last of my granddaddy's family besides me, and I guess besides my mama, wherever she is. Granddaddy said Aunt Mazel would sit with us anyway, and Aunt Sarah didn't say a word, though you could tell she wanted to real bad.

I wonder where my mama is right now. The letter says she will always be nearby; maybe she is just a few towns over, in Cotton Plant or Blue Mountain. If she is anywhere near here, she might know about Nana dying. She could even be right here somewhere. Of course, she might not be sad that her own mama died. She might not want to come to her own mama's funeral. Or maybe she is not even in Mississippi anymore. If I were going to go far away, I'd go to Arizona or California.

Before the service starts, I lean in close to my grand-daddy and ask, "Do you know everybody? Is there any-one here that looks new to you?" I am smashed in between Granddaddy and Aunt Sarah. She puts her hand on my leg to get me to stop talking. Without even look-ing around, Granddaddy shakes his head no.

"Do you think my mama possibly could be here?" I am careful to whisper this especially softly so that Aunt Sarah doesn't hear. She puts her hand back on me and gives my knee a tight squeeze. That's the church equiva-lent of giving me a little pop. I know she won't come out and pop me at my own nana's funeral, but this knee squeezing is supposed to have the same effect. I brush her hand off like it's a pesky fly. Granddaddy looks right at me with his red eyes, not knowing what to say, maybe, or not wanting to think about the possibility of her being here and then finding that she is not. He says finally, "No, dolly. I don't think she's here."

"Will you just look? Please?"

He turns and looks all around the church, even up into the choir loft. When his eyes stop in the very back, I hope for a few seconds that he has seen somebody new and different from all of these people that he has known for so long. I hope he will see somebody whose face looks as familiar as his own, and while he tries hard to remember who she is, she will see him, too. I pray hard for my mother to come out of the crowd and join us. He must wish her here, too.

"I'm sorry," he says after a while. "She's not here. She's probably far away and doesn't know."

I slip my hand in Granddaddy's to comfort him and me both. There's lots of crying, but none of it is from me. My tears are all dried up. Most of my crying I did right before Nana died, after our argument. I usually cry a lot, anyway. And the truth is that I like crying. I mean, I don't just sit around and cry for no reason. But when I have a reason, and lately it does seem like there have been more good reasons than usual, I just let myself cry, hard as I like. It's good, because crying like that makes me know I'm still real and still alive. I like the feeling, too, of using tears to get the pain out of me instead of letting it grow so big, like it did inside Nana, and I guess like it did inside of my mama. After a good long cry, I sleep hard, too, because I'm exhausted in that inside-outside way.

Even while Nana and I were arguing, I had had a feeling nothing would be the same, but I ignored that feeling by going to sleep. I hate it that we didn't find a way to make up. I wonder if Nana thought of that while she was dying. Or maybe she came in from cutting the grass to make up with me. She didn't finish the yard, so that could be it. She had finished the backyard and got as far as the day-lily bed around front. Maybe Nana was coming in to take a break and talk with me. It could be that she tried to call out, "Georgia Tate, Georgia Tate," but nothing came out.

I cut the rest of the yard this morning, before we came to church. Aunt Sarah kept hollering at me to come in and get dressed. I just ignored her like the lawn mower was too loud to hear over.

Everybody keeps saying Nana looks good. She looks good, but she doesn't look like herself. She looks too poofy. Also, she is wearing way more makeup than usual. They even put eye shadow on her, and red lipstick. Nana never wore red lipstick. She always wore peach. She called it coral. It's Aunt Sarah who did all of the color coordinating of Nana. She picked the navy blue polka-dot dress that Nana only wore one time, to a meeting of the teachers' sorority.

The teachers' sorority members are all here, sitting together. All of the teachers from school, even the black ones are here. The Reverend Jones, from the black church off Highway 4 going toward Memphis, is here, too. I believe he is here out of respect to Granddaddy. He and Granddaddy Tate like to meet at Sister's Diner on the square and talk about the Bible and other preacher things.

I don't think Granddaddy listens to the service. Dr. Ellis, the preacher from Holly Springs, is doing the entire funeral, even the eulogy. Everybody expected Granddaddy to do it, or at least part of it, but he wouldn't. He kept saying, "Lucy was my wife. We were married nearly forty years."

I guess that's the thing about being a preacher—sort of like being a doctor. People think that there must be nothing else to your life. What Granddaddy is saying is that he is more than the preacher of this church. He is also a husband. I think his not participating in the funeral is the tenderest thing I have ever seen between him and Nana.

I don't listen to the service, either.

CHAPTER TWELVE

After the cemetery service, Granddaddy Tate puts his arm around my shoulder and says, "Let's go for a drive before we go home." So we drive out Highway 15, just like we used to do with Nana. It's a Sunday, so the factories aren't running and it seems like no one is out except for the two of us.

I know that everybody from church is gathering at our house with food made especially for this day, and for when Granddaddy and I are alone, without Nana. Somebody has probably even made that nasty three-bean salad.

I reckon we should be getting back there soon, but Aunt Mazel and Aunt Sarah are there, too, and they can take care of things for a bit.

My granddaddy looks tired and small, and he is quiet. He is always kind of quiet, but not like this. This quiet seems to be from some hollow place inside him that I have never seen before. He pulls the truck over into Green-Old-Field, the same field where Ginger says my mama was with me when she shot herself.

Right now, more than anything, I want to comfort my granddaddy and make him feel full again. Nana did so much for us to make a family and a home, and now we will have to do those things ourselves. Most of those things I already know how to do—cook meals, wash clothes, work the garden, organize. I have been doing these things alongside Nana for my whole life. Now I tell myself I will keep our home running.

I don't think I can keep up the mole killing, though. I figure the moles, knowing Nana is dead, must be having a real celebration. They probably are already planning a big takeover of the garden.

Granddaddy interrupts my quiet and says, "When your mama was a little girl, we used to drive to this field. We would come to watch the sunset or eat ice-cream cones. Sometimes, we would race over here to catch the afternoon train so she could see the caboose. She loved to sing 'Little Red Caboose' and wave at the conductor on the back of the train. As she grew older, we would come here sometimes to talk, or just sit."

"Do you ever come here by yourself and think about my mama?"

"Every so often, I do. I used to come here almost every day. After a while, it got to be where that's all I wanted to do—come here and sit."

"So one day you just stopped coming?" I ask.

He nods, then says, "One day I realized that another little girl was counting on me." I want to hold him tight and never let go when he says this.

Instead, I close my eyes to imagine that I am my mama, here with Granddaddy—my daddy. I hear the train's whistle and can even taste the ice-cream cone—it's strawberry, and it drips down my hand because it is melting so fast. We sit together in the truck, the motor turned off, and the windows rolled down. The wind blows through the truck, carrying with it the smells of dirt and heat. I imagine that I sing the song Nana taught me:

Little Red Caboose-boose-boose-boose,
Coming down the track-track-track-track,
Smokestack on his back-back-back-back,
Little Red Caboose behind the train-train-train-train.

I wave at the train conductor.

Granddaddy interrupts my thinking again. "Monday week, you'll fly to Jacksonville to stay with your father and Sissy."

"*Stay* with them?" I ask.

"You're still a child, Georgia Tate," says Granddaddy. "You need a home where you can do all of the things a child is supposed to do—go to school, play outside, enjoy your friends, and not worry about adult things. You don't want to stay here and take care of me."

"Yes, I do. I do. I want to stay here and take care of both of us."

"Oh, dolly." My granddaddy sighs. "It's not that simple. It involves custody and who has a right to raise you."

"If I don't like it, I can come home, right?" I ask. He does what Nana used to do; he says nothing. A crack inside me starts and spreads to every part of me. I've got to make Granddaddy understand that I can't go down there to live. This is where I need to live, with him.

I remember hearing Nana tell Aunt Sarah that my daddy was threatening custody. I think he was trying to be all big and powerful. Right now, I want to be as powerful as everybody else, so I say, in my best and loudest smarty-pants voice, "I know what custody is and there is no court that would give my daddy custody! Nana said so herself!"

I am desperate to convince him, and so I call on Nana to help me.

This surprises him, I can tell, because his mouth drops open and his eyebrows shoot up.

"No, we're not going to court. We never have. We have always just agreed that you would live with us. Now you'll live with him."

In my mind, I plead with him and beg him, *Please! Please! Don't send me away!* In my mind, I chain myself to his ankle so that we are never apart and I cannot go away. In my mind, I fling my body in front of the train so I don't have to go. All of that happens in my mind, while I hang my face out the window on the drive home.

It seems like the entire town has brought food. There is more than one disgusting three-bean salad. The dining room, den, living room, and kitchen are entirely filled up with people, all of them saying Nana was a good woman.

I sit on the fireplace stoop, watching Granddaddy try to smile and nod his head thanks to all the visitors. At first, nobody says much to me, but I do catch a lot of the ladies looking at me and then whispering. They all seem to know already that I am leaving here. I bet my aunt Sarah blabbed it to everyone.

Some of the ladies from church try to talk to me and tell me it's the best thing for everybody. "Just give it some time—you'll see." I want to scream at them all, *No! You'll see! This is where I live! This is where I should stay!*

While they're still talking to me, I turn and run down the hall into my room, the only place in the house where I can be alone. When I was visiting my daddy before the Fourth of July, I knew that I would come home. Now it's different. It hurts too much to think about what it will be like, not being here. It's hard to do what Nana always said and find the good, because it seems to me that finding the good depends on whether or not there is hope. Even if you can't see something good right away, if you can hope for something good, then that's enough. Like this summer when I visited him, the best thing about it was that I knew I would come home. That's hope. I don't see any now, with me leaving here for good.

I close my eyes and try to find the sound of the clock ticking in the living room. There it is, past all the voices, the plates and forks clicking, the feet walking from room to room. There is the clock, keeping up with everything, as if nothing has changed at all.

CHAPTER THIRTEEN

On the airplane, I open the shoebox that Granddaddy gave me at the airport. It is not as good as the ones Nana used to fix me for long trips when I was little, but it's good because he fixed it for me. There are stamps, and envelopes pre-addressed to Reverend Aaron Samuel Tate. The list of everything I need to remember to do is in here, too—register for school, find a doctor, find a dentist, find a church, write home. There's some Doublemint gum (Granddaddy's favorite), a new hairbrush, barrettes, and an envelope, marked EMERGENCY, with two brand-new fifty-dollar bills inside.

There is even a romance novel from Ginger in the box. Ginger loves romance. She cleans stalls three days a week in exchange for free riding lessons. She wants to bounce on a horse and have the wind blow through her hair like in the books she reads. She even traces the pictures from the book covers with tracing paper and saves them. I have to say, I love that about Ginger: she just sees a picture in her mind, for only a second, of how she wants to be, and the next thing you know, there she is, right in front of you. Even though she's just learning to ride, she already looks like she ought to be on the cover of one of those books. Her hair is long and blond, her skin is brown as a pancake from swimming all summer, and her chest is so big and sits up so proud. She hates wearing a riding helmet when she's on the horse. She thinks it interferes with how good she looks. It does, too, because you don't get the full effect of hair flowing. I will really miss Ginger. Everything in this box makes me cry about leaving here and about never seeing Nana again. I put the letter from my mama in the box, too, so that everything important is all there together.

When my daddy picks me up at the airport, he surprises me with a pink box with a pink Cinderella watch inside. It is the most beautiful watch I have ever had. Really, it's the only watch I've ever had. Nana bought me an alarm clock for school last year because, she said, it was time I started getting up on my own every day. I told her I didn't need an alarm, because she always sets the big clock every morning after it winds down at night, and it starts bonging right at six. She'd said, "Some morning I may not be here, so you need to get in the habit of waking yourself at the same time every day, on your own. A clock will help build a good habit." I reckon she was right.

PART TWO

I go back into the water and swim all the way under, to the very bottom. It goes on for what seems forever, and near the bottom is a hole wide enough to swim through. There is a black dolphin, much bigger than I am, waiting for me. I grab on to her, and she takes me out through the bottom of the river. It is a fantastic place to be, swimming with her. I am all the way underwater, breathing fine and flying. I hold on tight to her, and I never want to let go. Soon we come up for air, and we are in the ocean. There are no people here, only dolphins and other animals. The sand is white-white, and the water is bluer than in any picture I have ever seen. The dolphin stays nearby while I walk along the beach.

CHAPTER FOURTEEN

Most days, I go to work with my daddy. He manages a hotel on the outside of town. He thinks the most important thing that I should do before school is to get a Florida suntan. Although I have my own guest room to hang out in, he makes me sit by the pool all day long. The first week I was here, I got sunburned so bad that my whole face puffed up like the snake man at the state fair back home. Even after I showed my daddy how red I was getting, he just said it would turn brown in a couple of days. But then my eyes swelled shut, and I couldn't see. My daddy was scared enough that he took me to the doctor. I got some little pills to take down the swelling, and, thankfully, the doctor said I shouldn't stay out in the sun so much. A few days later, I peeled even worse than a snake.

My daddy also thinks I should lose weight, so he doesn't like for me to eat very much. He keeps saying, "Before you start school, you're going to be suntanned and twenty pounds lighter." I have lost eleven pounds since I have been here. When I look in the mirror now, the girl I see doesn't look like Georgia Tate Jamison. If you ask me, I didn't need to lose even one pound, because I was just right when I first got here—not too fat and not too skinny, but just what an outdoor girl like me should be.

I am supposed to weigh myself every morning and write down on a chart what the scale says. I don't ever eat breakfast, and once he even gave me a whipping for eating two candy bars in a row. Not counting being popped, which was usually for saying something smart, Nana only whipped me one time in my whole life. That was when I got caught going to J.D.'s.

Last summer, Ginger and I were in town, walking around the square like always. Ginger had been bragging about how good she was at Galaxy, which we usually played at the pizza place on Highway 15. She knew they had a Galaxy machine at J.D.'s pool hall, which is just one block off the square, across from the jail. She talked me into going there and playing against her. There were only a couple of men in there, and they didn't say anything to us while we played. It didn't seem like that bad of a place to me.

But the minute I got home, Nana had the switch waiting. She made me pull my panties down, and she was four switches into it before I had even figured out what I had done wrong. Maybe because J.D.'s is just down the street from the jail is why she got so mad. Mrs. Clayton Thomas is the one who called Nana up and told her that Ginger and I were coming out of J.D.'s, laughing and cutting up. After that, Nana wouldn't let me have anything to do with Ginger Parsons for a while. She said Ginger was a bad influence on me, and that I ought to know better than to make friends with a girl whose mama let her run around town barefoot.

I know that Nana would whip me something fierce if she saw me right now. Not only am I in a bar, but I am wearing a pair of Sissy's red high heels. When my daddy first handed them to me, I was nervous about whether I could even walk in them or not. My Sunday school shoes don't have a heel at all, and even Nana's high heels are not like these small, pointy ones.

We are at the Cock N Bull, where most nights my daddy and I go for dinner after Sissy goes to work. We end up staying until it closes. He doesn't like to eat in the restaurant part, so we sit in the bar. When we go out, he likes me to wear makeup and dress up in Sissy's clothes, which truthfully I think are too revealing.

Tonight I am wearing one of Sissy's dresses, and my hair is curled real big like Charlie's Angels. To me, I look at least twenty-five. There is no one in the bar except the two of us, the waitress, and the bartender. The waitress is always especially nice to me. Once, when I saw her in the bathroom, she told me in the nicest way that I needed to fix my blush. We were standing at the sink and I could see her just staring at me.

"Sweetheart, your blush is a pretty color on you. Want me to show you a trick about blending it in?" Her voice was so quiet that what I really wanted her to do was to take all of this makeup off. I nodded.

"You want to try to make the line between the blush and your face almost invisible. You have the right idea. Here, let me soften it up for you." She took a piece of toilet paper and dabbed at my cheek and then used her thumb to rub the blush in a little more. When she was holding my chin, looking to see if it was right, I wanted to hug her.

"There, that's much better. You're lucky; you have such a pretty face that you don't need so much makeup as the rest of us do. What do you think? Isn't that a better look for you?" I looked in the mirror and had to admit that it was nicer.

Tonight when we leave the Cock N Bull, he is more drunk than usual, so I have to drive. When Granddaddy used to let me drive his truck back home, it was easier because it was an automatic. Now I grind the gears the whole way, and the engine keeps cutting off because it's hard to let the clutch out in just the right way. By the time we arrive, I have gotten pretty good at the clutch part, but it's still hard to find the gears.

I want to die when I see Sissy's car in the driveway. Everything I'm wearing is hers—her dress, her shoes, her makeup, even her little purse. It's what he told me to do, but I know that she will hate it. My mama's letter is in the purse, because I carry it everywhere with me, so just in case, I take the letter out and tuck it into my bra.

My daddy is passed out next to me. His shoes are off, and his feet are the smelliest of any I have ever been around. I don't have even a minute to worry about waking him up, because Sissy is out the door and at the truck before I have even figured out how to get the keys out of the ignition. She is madder than a dirt dauber.

"Ray, get out of the goddamn truck." She opens the door and pulls him out. "Get your sorry ass out of my truck."

When he lands on the driveway, that wakes him up.

"I love you, Sissy," he says.

This sets her off.

"You *love* me? You don't love anybody but yourself, Rayford. I'm a joke to you, you arrogant son of a bitch. I'm just the girl who sucks your dick."

"What's the goddamn problem, Sissy. Couldn't find your boyfriend tonight? Is that why you're home so early?"

Now Sissy looks over at me and I know he could not have said anything worse. This will, in a second, get very bad, and even though I am just sitting here, she is going to make this all my fault. And she does.

"Ray, go on inside. Go on inside and fuck your daughter. Give me my fucking truck keys, and you go fuck your daughter."

I know exactly what "fuck" means. I'm sure Nana and Granddaddy Tate would think I have never even heard the word, but I know because Ginger told me. My daddy and Sissy always say it, and the thought of what it is is gross to me. It is especially gross to think about him. Not just because of his stinky feet, but because of how he makes me dress up in Sissy's stuff and then looks at me. But I know Sissy is right, that he wants to do that to me. I just try to keep those thoughts out of my mind.

"Georgia Tate?" She is saying my name and I can't do anything except sit here and wish her away. "Georgia Tate? Who do you think you are? Get out of my dress."

"Okay. I'll go inside and take it off." I start to get out of the truck.

"No, take it off now. You are wearing my goddamn dress, and I want it." She is on my side of the truck now, with the door open. He is leaning on the hood, watching.

"I'd rather take it off inside and give it right back," I say in as nice a way as anybody could.

"Take it off *now,* so we can watch you."

So I take the dress off in the driveway. She didn't ask for the shoes, but they are hers, too, so I hand them to her first. I am so glad that I don't have on her black bra and panties that he told me to wear. I have never felt so happy before about disobeying someone. I can only think how awful it would be to be standing here in her driveway wearing her bra and underwear. She would make me take those off, too, and that would make me die.

"Ray, come watch your daughter undress for you."

"Sissy, stop it, baby," he says. He walks over to her and puts his arm around her waist. "Come here. Let's make up."

He actually tries to kiss her, and I know this is a mistake. She slaps him, and he doesn't say anything. Except, after it stings, he punches her way harder than she hit him. Then he just walks inside.

I am halfway naked, in my own panties and bra, looking at Sissy all curled up in the driveway. She is crying without any noise and something makes me want to hold her. Maybe it is the strength and love I feel from my mama's letter, tucked away safe inside my bra and close to my heart, that makes my own heart feel kind toward her. I sit down beside her and put my arms around her. "Sissy, are you okay? I'm sorry he hit you so hard. Are you okay?"

"Georgia Tate, go inside and pack your stuff. You are not staying in my home."

What I want right now, more than anything, is to go back to the last day I saw Nana. I hadn't really thought of having honey buns for breakfast with her on that morning. But as soon as I smelled them and heard her in the kitchen, I could hardly get in there fast enough. What I had wanted to do was to sit right up next to her, like I always had done, and stay in my nightgown, cuddling her and being quiet and together.

Right now I want to close my eyes and be back at home. I want to be with Nana.

it and sprayed it with disinfectant. It's awfully hard to fall asleep on it, because all it takes is one thought of one little roach and I feel them crawling all over me. Then I turn on the light and see that they really are not crawling on me; it's just in my mind. The roaches aren't even the worst part of the sofa. It's full of fleas. They eat me alive every single night, and that is not my imagination. I scratch my legs so bad in my sleep that they are always bleeding in the morning. Nana used to tell me that scratching mosquito bites scars up your legs for life.

This sofa is not a sleep sofa like the one at home. I cover the sofa with a sheet that I brought with me, and at least that way my skin's not touching the actual infested sofa cushions.

At first, this place was an awful mess, worse than anything I've ever seen. I have to say that now it's really not that bad. What is most embarrassing is that he reads dirty magazines. It was hard at first not to look at them, so I did, and some of the stuff in there I just could not believe, both the pictures and the writing. I mean, I have heard most of those words before, from him and also from Ginger. I wonder, does he think in those words about me when he starts wanting me to get all dressed up and go out with him or looking at me in that way? I didn't say anything at all to him about the magazines; I just stacked them up in a paper grocery bag and put them in his bedroom. He didn't say anything about that or about how clean everything is now.

We use a card table to eat on; it's usually stacked with my daddy's beer cans and our McDonald's bags from breakfast and lunch. There is a McDonald's just down the street and a Dollar Store sort of catty-corner to us, which is good to have.

Something is wrong with the electricity in this place, because only one wall outlet works. When we got here, it was so hot and humid that we were alternating running the air conditioner and turning the lamp on, because only the single outlet could be used. I bought one of those things you plug into the wall to get more plug space out of it. So now we can run the lamp, the air conditioner, and the radio all at one time. I think that's the smartest thing I've ever done.

The whole trip to the Dollar Store worked out just fine. I had to spend about thirty of the one hundred dollars that Granddaddy gave me, but it seemed worth it, to make the place a little nicer. I also bought a Scrabble game, a pretty blue tablecloth for the card table, a wooden rack for drying dishes, and some coat hangers, so I could hang my other clothes in the hall closet. I got good deals on everything, and I bet this apartment is cleaner now than it ever has been.

I found an old beat-up bike laying beside the Dumpster

in the alley out back and spent a little bit more of my money fixing it up. I spray-painted it white, so it looks real nice. There was a rip in the seat, so I just wrapped a lot of black duct tape around it. I couldn't resist getting a straw basket for the front, and then I bought a chain and lock, so that no one can steal it. I have to ride to the gas station and put air in the tires every couple of days, but that is not a big deal, because the air is free and having the bike makes it easy to get almost anywhere, especially the library.

The library here is way bigger than even the court-house at home, and there are forty-two steps just to get to the front door. It has three floors and a basement, all full of books and tapes and magazines, and one room with chairs so soft they make me fall asleep.

Last week I got a talking-to by one of the librarians, about sleeping in the library. The not-so-nice librarian is the one I mean. Everything about her is pointy: her hair, her nose, her chin—even her shoes. She told me that if I could not stay awake, then I couldn't come into the library anymore. The other librarian never says a word to me about sleeping in those chairs. She just smiles at me and says whatever books I'm checking out look interest-ing. It's not like I go in there intending to fall asleep. I go in there intending to read, because there are some things, like the magazines, they don't let you take home. I always tell myself to sit in a hard wooden chair by the air conditioner so I'll stay awake, but my body doesn't listen. I'll be telling myself, the whole way into that comfortable room, not to go in there because it's too cozy, and then before I know it, I am curled up in one of those chairs, drooling so much that it wakes me up. That room is also perfect for sleeping because of the way the sun comes right in on me. I feel like a cat when I'm in that room.

CHAPTER SIXTEEN

We float in an inner tube down a river near Gainesville, Florida. I am wearing a silver bikini that used to belong to Sissy. The bottoms are too small, the top is too big, and most of me isn't covered up very well. He is smoking, not a cigarette, but what he calls a joint. It smells sweeter than his Marlboros; so I don't mind so much breathing it in. He tells me to jump in the river and give in to the water. So I do.

I can't breathe because the water is so cold and forceful. My chest hurts, and I am so afraid—of what is in here and that I will drown—that I can't move. The water is deep and black. I want to cry, but he thinks girls are babies, so I don't.

The river is strong and it pulls me under. When I bob up, he is laughing at me and the inner tube is faraway. It starts to rain. He disappears around a bend, and now I do cry. I cry hard because I am so mad and so afraid. Finally, I give in and the river supports me. I can see the inner tube parked under a tree along the bank. He is partially hidden by Spanish moss hanging so low that it touches the water. His long, tan legs dangle over the side of the inner tube. I see him light another joint.

I swim up to the inner tube, panting with relief and exhaustion. There is a field of rain hiding us under the tree. He offers me the joint and I shake my head no and push his hand away. My eyes close, and my head, grateful for a break from the rapids, rests on the tube. My thighs burn. I look down to find the fire that has dropped from the joint—it is his hand. It easily slips under my bikini. I say, "Stop it," but he does not. He pushes open my legs. I keep my eyes closed so this will not be real. I have to go to the bathroom and I want to die. He pushes his tongue down into my mouth.

I hear voices coming down the river toward us. We say nothing and do not look at each other. The inner tube takes us down the river into a wide, warm swimming hole where we are no longer alone.

CHAPTER SEVENTEEN

There's an old Haitian woman, Marie-Bernard, who lives upstairs with her grandson. He's three. She calls him Freedom, but everyone else calls him J.J., because his real name is Jean-Jacques. He is a funny little guy, because he will only answer me if I call him J.J. If I call him Freedom, he acts like he doesn't even hear me. He only hears that name when Marie-Bernard calls him.

I met her last week because two boys stole her purse right from her hands, in the middle of the day. I was coming home from the library on my bike, and I saw Marie-

Bernard waving her arms and these two boys running toward me very fast. I knew that something was wrong. I had this urge to pull my bike up into them to make them stop, but I didn't. I didn't see her purse, or I probably would have. The two boys ran right past me, so close that I could practically taste their sweat.

I've had that happen before—the feeling of doing nothing in the middle of something terrible. It's a strange feeling. I get so scared that I freeze up on the outside and kind of go off into my own world on the inside. That sort of happened with these boys. I could smell and feel that they were panting like dogs. But I couldn't say or do one thing. I rode up to the old woman. "Are you okay?" I asked.

"I'm fine, but they stole my purse."

"You go call the police," I said, and I took off chasing them on my bike. I never caught them, but I know they saw me, because they kept looking back. Finally I stopped and turned around because they were going into a neighborhood that I've never been in, and I got a little scared. I don't know what I was planning to do if I had caught up to them—except maybe be scared again.

When I got back to our building, Marie-Bernard was sitting on the stoop, crying because all of her money for the whole month was in the purse. All of her money for rent, for food, and for lights and water was in there. We called the police, and they came and got descriptions from me and from Marie-Bernard. They told me not to do anything stupid like chase robbers on my bike again. The police said that the boys probably had a gun and could have shot me. I never thought of that; I just thought that it's not right to take an old lady's purse. And it made me mad as heck that they did it right in the middle of the day—just came up and snatched it out of her hand—and they probably didn't even think a thing about it. That's why I chased them, to make them think about that they might get caught. At least maybe next time, they won't come back here.

Marie-Bernard and I are sort of becoming friends because of her pocketbook being stolen. I am a little bit worried about her. Yesterday I went upstairs to check on her, and she was just sitting in a chair in the dark. The electric company turned her lights out because she couldn't pay her bill. I don't know how all of that is supposed to work, but it seems awfully mean of them to do that. It seemed like the right thing to do to help Marie-Bernard with her overdue bill. I gave her the rest of my money, except I kept back ten dollars for myself in case of an emergency. It wasn't enough to pay the whole amount, but it was enough to get the power back on.

I invited Marie-Bernard and J.J. to come down and

eat with me. Marie-Bernard wouldn't eat very much. But J.J. ate more than I did. Nana would have been upset with me for having black people in the house. She was funny that way. Granddaddy is not that way, and I think that it caused some trouble for him with Nana.

Last year in social studies, we had to interview someone about the civil rights movement and write a paper about what we learned. We were supposed to interview someone who had lived through that time. I started out interviewing Granddaddy Tate, because he had a church in Selma, Alabama, in the fifties and right up until he was called to serve at our church in Ripley. I expected him to say that he preached a lot about civil rights and walked in the protests, because I knew that many white ministers in Alabama and Mississippi did help make the changes. But Granddaddy was not one of them.

I quoted him word for word in my paper. He said, "I was reared in Alabama, and for my whole life, the races did not intermix; we believed that was the natural way. I never questioned that or thought much about it until I was a chaplain in World War Two. We were stationed in Guam, where the black soldiers and white soldiers worshiped separately, but there was no black chaplain. I was chaplain for all of the men. The first time I gave Communion to a black man, God humbled me and ripped away my pride. Here I was the chaplain for hundreds of men, yet the faith of these men was stronger and deeper than my own faith. I could see it in their faces full of joy, hear it in their tear-filled song, and feel that the Holy Spirit was present with us during these services. We were worshiping the same God, in the same way, yet they believed more fully than I in God's promise."

I asked him why he didn't do anything in Selma if he understood things differently after the war. He cried. He cried and he hid his face in his hands. Finally, he said, "If there is one mistake that I have made as a minister, it is that I didn't do more in Selma. But I was scared."

I was interviewing him while Nana was driving us around, showing us a new house out by the country club. "You would've lost your church, too. You ought to be glad, too, that you didn't do anything," she said.

He told me that he had preached one Sunday sermon about civil rights—just one. After that, the Board of Deacons called him in for a conference and told him not to stir things up by preaching like that again. They told him to preach the Gospel, not make trouble with "the nigras." Granddaddy told them that the Gospel is clear that we are all brothers in Christ. My granddaddy walked out of that meeting. Later that night, some men burned a cross in the front yard of the manse.

When I interviewed Granddaddy, he suggested that I

also interview Reverend DeWitt Jones. Reverend Jones is the custodian at my old school. I call him Reverend Jones because he also is a pastor like my granddaddy. He is the preacher at one of the black churches outside of town; there aren't any black churches in town.

We went to Reverend Jones's house together on a Saturday morning, after we had finished all of our errands. I don't think Nana knew that's where we were.

Reverend Jones lives at the very end of Union Street. I have visited folks on Union Street with Granddaddy before, but never on Reverend Jones's end. When we pulled up, some boys were playing kickball in the street, and some girls were drawing pictures on the sidewalk with chalk. I recognized Duane Johnson from my class and I waved at him. He barely waved back. In fact, when my granddaddy and I got out of the truck, all of the children stopped playing and kind of disappeared. It was real weird. They must not get many white people coming through.

Four of us—me, Granddaddy, Reverend Jones, and Reverend Jones's mother-in-law—sat in the living room, talking for an hour or more. The mother-in-law didn't really talk. She just watched television that was so loud that we all had to shout over top of it to be heard. The truth is, I don't think the mother-in-law even knew that they had company. Two pictures hung above the television set, one of Jesus and the other of Dr. Martin Luther

King Jr. It felt sort of strange looking at a white Jesus in a black man's house. It made me wonder what color of skin Jesus really had. He was from Israel, which I think is over near Egypt and Africa, so his skin was probably more brownish than anything.

When I asked Reverend Jones if he had ever preached about civil rights, he just laughed at me, like was I serious. So I asked him again.

"I still preach about it, young lady, every week in the pulpit, every day in my conversations with my flock, with people like you, and your grandfather. The true meaning of the Gospel of the Lord Jesus Christ is all about God's unconditional love for each and every one of us—and God's desire that we love one another in that way, as well. No matter what the color of our skin or our rank in life. Do you understand what I'm saying?"

I did, and it made good sense to me. Reverend Jones didn't seem the least bit scared about it.

"Were you scared you would lose your church?" I asked.

"Georgia Tate, what does Jesus say about losing the things of this world?"

"Well, I think he said something like you have to lose your life to get your life." I was hoping that I was pretty close on this.

"That's right! So am I scared? Yes! There are many days and nights when I am scared. But fear does not propel me into action or paralyze me. Love and the righteousness of God—they are what move me."

I asked him if things have changed since then, and in some ways he seemed to get angry at that question, too. He said, "We integrated the schools, so they built a new private school on the west side of the county. We integrated the city pool and community center—finally, our children had something to do and some place to cool off during the hot summer. But they built the country club. We began to walk on the sidewalks, instead of in the street. We began to shop in the same stores on the square where the white families had shopped for years. So they moved their stores far out on Highway 15, so you'd have to own a car to have access. We integrated the football, basketball, and baseball teams. At first, they wouldn't let our children start. At least we've gotten beyond that one. But the truth is, the civil rights movement all but bypassed this county. Black teachers and coaches are still paid less; the factories that are left hire black people to work the line, and white people to oversee their work; and there has yet to be a black principal or black representative on the Board of Supervisors. White children call me 'Nigger' or 'DeWitt,' because to them, respect for their elders means

127

respect for white elders. Every year, when the marching band travels to Washington, D.C., to represent the state of Mississippi, there is still at least one white child who cries and complains to come home because he or she has to share a room with a black child. And the law, the law in this county, is the law of the white man. So am I scared? Yes, every day of my life I am scared. Does this stop me? No, there is much to be done, even now, even today."

I ended up getting an A-plus on my paper, I think because I talked to two different people, and not too long after that, Granddaddy and Reverend Jones started a preacher swap. That's where the preachers switch congregations for one Sunday. I think that day was the beginning of a nice friendship between the two of them.

Marie-Bernard wasn't even in this country when civil rights were starting. J.J. was a brand-new baby when they came to America. I love to watch him sometimes while Marie-Bernard runs errands. Not for pay, but because I don't really have anything else to do, and it's easier for Marie-Bernard to run errands or do her business without J.J. When she goes to church at night or to visit friends, I go over there and stay with him. Her place is nicer than ours, and it's fun to babysit. I think his personality is what Nana used to always call "an easy baby," even though he is not really a baby.

He doesn't talk yet, at least not in English and not even much in Creole. By his eyes and his smile, you can tell that everything is okay with him. By that I mean he is not slow, or anything—he just doesn't talk. He works puzzles, goes to the bathroom on his own, gets dressed by himself, and draws beautiful pictures of everything and everyone around him. Marie-Bernard says he doesn't talk because he saw his mother killed in Haiti and the spirits have taken away his voice. "Enough love will heal and restore his voice" is what she says. So maybe it's good for me to be around to give him some extra love on top of Marie-Bernard's.

J.J. will sit in my lap forever while I read to him, and he doesn't get into anything, ever. I love it when he smiles. We'll be just sitting on the sofa, reading, and he will look up at me and smile and touch my face, and it makes me want to cry.

Sometimes I sing to him. "Amazing Grace" seems to be his favorite, and it reminds me of Granddaddy, so I like singing that one. J.J. likes for me to sing when he is falling asleep. I just sing it over and over, sometimes fifteen or twenty times. If I stop too soon, he pops his head up and sort of nods for me to keep going. I use different words than most people do, because I don't like the part about "saved a wretch like me." Once I heard someone else sing that part "saved and set me free." So that's the way I've been singing "Amazing Grace" ever since. I think it fits better for J.J., anyway. How can a small child be a wretch?

Across the hall from us, there are always a bunch of boys who I think go to college. I don't know who lives there and who doesn't, but there are always six or seven of them being loud and playing music and stuff. I try to ignore them because I don't think they are very nice. Mostly, they ignore me, too, and they ignore Marie-Bernard. There also is a woman—well, really a man—who lives upstairs and across the hall from Marie-Bernard. The boys downstairs are very mean to her. In the day-time, she wears a bandanna over her hair, just like Marie-Bernard does, only with curlers underneath. She always has a cigarette in one hand and a Tab in the other. Except at night—then she looks like a movie star.

Yesterday, when she was coming in with groceries, one of the downstairs boys flicked a cigarette butt at her and said, "Hey, Tamika, how's business?"

She said, "Fuck you, midget-prick," and kept on going. That made me laugh right out loud, and the guy across the hall turned red in the face when he saw me. That's when he first paid any attention to me, when he got all embarrassed. He looked at me and said, "I don't have a midget prick." Tamika heard him and shouted down,

"Your girlfriend says so." Those boys are always calling Tamika "faggot" and "drag queen." I had heard almost all those words before, or read them in the magazines my daddy leaves around. But "drag queen" I had not heard.

There is something very sweet and soft about Tamika, even though she really is a boy. Some days she wears a shower cap over her curlers instead of the bandanna. And even though her face sometimes needs shaving first thing in the morning, her legs never do. I have made a special point of looking at her legs because I have just started shaving mine. It seems like every day I have some little black hairs popping up and making them feel all prickly. But Tamika's legs always look as smooth as J.J.'s skin. During the day, Tamika is always home, and she doesn't have any breasts. At night when she is usually real dressed up, she has nice round breasts, rounder and bigger than mine. Not that mine are that big, but I am a real girl, so I'd expect mine to be a little more real looking, but they're not. In fact, at night Tamika is about the prettiest woman I have ever seen, prettier even than Sissy.

She doesn't speak to me; she kind of ignores me, just like the boys across the hall do. Marie-Bernard says that Tamika is not natural. In fact, Marie-Bernard doesn't even call her Tamika. She calls her Robert. "That is a young man, and his name is Robert. I know because I get the

CHAPTER EIGHTEEN

Every day I tell God that I need to get home, and I tell Him that my granddaddy needs to get some sense about this and finally bring me back to Ripley. There are so many things that I hate about living here, and I have never truly hated anything before now. I hate that my daddy has special outfits that I'm supposed to wear out with him. I hate how he makes me dance with him, and that when we dance, he pulls me close and breathes on my neck. I hate the way he sings in my ear. But what I hate the most about living here is looking trashy like those girls in his magazines. It might sound strange, but I only do it so he will leave me alone. Most of the time it's enough for him that I dress up and pretend to date him.

I try to block my mind from wondering what people who see me like this must think of me. I know what Nana would think of someone like me when I'm out with him. I don't know what my mama would think. I have a feeling she might understand, and I wish she was here to take me away. I tell that to God, too, and I ask Him to fix things so she'll come back soon.

On nights like tonight, I do what he says for two reasons. One: I don't feel as afraid of him in public as I do at the apartment. Two: the longer we stay out dancing, the more he drinks, and I want him to get drunk enough to leave me alone, drunk enough that all he can do is sleep. Then I can drive him home. Sometimes I leave him passed out in the truck. Sometimes I have to help him into the house and then hope he will forget I am there and keep to himself.

When I'm at the library or with Marie-Bernard and J.J., I can mostly forget about nights like this. He has not touched me anywhere or done anything since that last time we were at the river, but I can tell that he wants to.

There is nothing really different about tonight. We go to the same place and he orders the same drink—scotch on the rocks with a splash. Our same waitress is here; she winks at me when I order a cheeseburger and fries. He drinks even more than usual, and so I drive home. I'm good at driving a stick shift now, and I am careful to do everything right so any policemen around won't be tempted to pull me over.

I hope that by the time we're back, I can just leave him in the truck and go on in by myself. I need a good night's sleep because tomorrow I am getting up early and riding my bike all the way across town to the hot-air balloon show at the airport. I have already pumped the tires of my bike and packed my lunch. The airport is about twelve miles away, which should be a piece of cake to do in around an hour.

The balloons are scheduled to go up at nine o'clock, and I want to be there in plenty of time. I'll probably leave around seven-thirty, so that means getting up before seven to shower and eat. Even if I were already asleep right now, I'd still be a little short of a good night. But that's okay.

We pull up to the building and he is not asleep. At the apartment door, he fumbles and drops the keys, then tells me, "Open it."

I open the door and right away start making up the sofa. He goes into his room in the dark, and I can hear him just sitting there.

"Georgia Tate? Come in here."

I wait a few minutes, still wishing he will pass out.

"Georgia Tate! I need your help."

I don't answer him, but I go in. He is sitting on the edge of the bed all dressed, except he has taken his shoes off. "Come sit by me. Help me get these pants off. I'm drunk."

I say nothing, and I make no move to help him, thinking to myself, How will I ever get out of this?

He yells, "Do it!" So I start helping him out of his clothes. I pretend that I am a nurse and that he is a really sick, really old patient of mine. Nurses probably have a way of undressing men patients so that the men don't get any funny ideas. They are probably very businesslike. So I am very businesslike. I don't look at him in the face. I think about humming, but that might seem like I am having too much fun, so I silently get him down to his boxer shorts and turn to leave.

"You're not finished."

"I am finished. You do the rest."

He pulls me down beside him again and puts his hand behind my hair. "You know you're the only woman who really loves me."

"I'm a girl, Dad. I'm not a woman."

"Are you still a virgin?" he asks.

And it all turns bad now. Before I can answer, he pushes his hand up under my skirt and yanks my panties way down. I don't do anything, because he is hurting me enough to show me that he could hurt me a lot more if he wanted. He half crawls and half falls on top of me. He is shoving his hands and mouth everywhere and talking to me and asking me questions while he does everything. He stinks like scotch and cigarettes.

I want to be asleep and I want to be alone. It is dark in here, like being inside of a box or a car trunk or maybe a casket. After a few minutes, I don't hear or smell him anymore.

I am in the calm, warm, summer ocean. There are a million or more stars out tonight, so close that I could reach up and rearrange them if they weren't already perfect. There is only ocean wind, and no clouds or storms are anywhere. There are no birds; only waves rolling in. I don't roll with them; I stay floating in one spot while the waves roll right over me. There is nothing in the ocean except me. There are no sharks or jellyfish to make me afraid and no dolphins to keep me safe. There is only me in the water, looking at the stars. I think, too, that

137

though I am alone, God is probably in the stars

somewhere, too. I try to think of something to say

to God, but there is nothing to say.

I feel wet and dizzy. Dizzy now because I'm unsure where I am, and why I am not really at the ocean, or maybe I am already asleep. My eyes have adjusted to the room enough to see him roll off of me.

"You can go now," he says, and then, "I pulled out." I don't ask what that means. In the bathroom I can see that the wet I felt was my own blood. I clean up as best I can and fix my skirt and panties. Then I go back to my sofa in the living room. It's easy to fall asleep after this, and I don't dream.

CHAPTER NINETEEN

I wake up late and I hurt. The blood is all dried and brown now, and there isn't any more than last night, so it must not be my period. Ginger, in her letters to me, keeps asking if I've started yet.

It's already eight o'clock.

I had planned for today to be my first perfect day here.

At the county airport, which really is more like just a field, there is a big air show today. I am going to ride my bike there and take a hot-air balloon ride.

Usually on Sundays, I ride my bike around all day long. I have not set foot in a church once since I got here. Sometimes when I am thinking about home, and especially about Granddaddy Tate, it turns out to be during church time. Then I wonder what he is preaching about and whether or not he is praying about me. He probably thinks everything is fine here because I haven't written to tell him it's not.

I keep meaning to write to Granddaddy, but I am waiting to have one perfect day when I can write him about everything that happens. Granddaddy writes me every week, sometimes even two or three times a week. He tells me everything about home and everything about my cousins and my friends. Ginger Parsons and her mama have started coming to Granddaddy's church because Ginger's mom got married again, this time to a Presbyterian, one of the McCanns. Even though he is part of the McCanns who run the funeral parlor, he doesn't take care of the dead bodies. He owns two dry cleaners, one in town and one in Falkner, and they pick up and deliver for the same price as the other one, so I guess he is on the road a lot. Ginger's mom is always helping him, even on Saturdays, so Ginger is really having a big time; it sounds like she is basically living all by herself. They don't have the Habitat House anymore; now they live in town.

I bet even Nana would like Ginger a lot now. Nana

was funny like that; she cared a lot about where someone lived or attended church. But I know that living in a nice house in town and going to Granddaddy's church, even though Granddaddy is the best preacher anywhere in the world, would not change Ginger Parsons. To Ginger, there is no such thing as bad or wrong. It's all just here for us to try. To Ginger, everything is an adventure. For example, she'll eat anything—she told me that once when she was shopping in Memphis, which is a bigger deal than shopping in Tupelo or New Albany, she ordered fried alligator meat from a restaurant in the mall. Well, that's just disgusting to me. She's also got it bad for every boy she's ever seen, and she wants to try everything there is to try with boys, too.

I imagine that, in some ways, God probably really likes that about Ginger. She's just so into everything, and He created everything, so He's probably pretty happy that at least somebody is out here appreciating the whole world. In all of her letters it sounds like her life is just fine.

Ginger is such a good friend that she writes me every week, too, even though I haven't written her either. Ginger is very nice about Granddaddy's preaching in her letters to me. She even tells me when Granddaddy talks about me in his sermons sometimes. He's always worked golf and fishing into his preaching, but I've never heard him work me in. That's nice.

She says that sometimes my granddaddy comes over to her house after church on Sundays, now that they are Presbyterians. Ginger says his preaching is as good as always, but that in real life, when he's not in the pulpit, he seems sadder than an old dog. In her last letter, she said that he almost cried at the table when Ginger said she had not received one word from me at all.

Granddaddy is funny about long-distance calls. He did call me one time; it was last week, but I wasn't home. My daddy talked to him and told him that I am doing fine. He also told him that I am learning to drive and that we are getting ready to buy me some new clothes for school in a couple of weeks. Well, Granddaddy is not stupid. I am sure that he knew that was a big hint for some money for my clothes. Granddaddy sent me a letter with a check made out to me for a hundred dollars. The letter said:

Dear Georgia Tate,

I miss you. Your daddy said you might need some new school clothes before long. I wish this check could be for more. I hear you are learning to drive. Write when you can and tell me all about it.

Love and miss you,
Granddaddy

Well, I can hardly write and tell him all about driving a drunk man around. I'm not learning how to drive; I am just damn driving because somebody has to. I won't write him about that; I will write him about the air show. I'll write him all about the dozens of balloons and how it feels to ride in a balloon and in a plane, because they will be giving free balloon and airplane rides all day long. I'll write Ginger about that, too; she'll like to hear about a real adventure. I know for a fact that Ginger has never seen or been in a hot-air balloon, and I don't believe that my granddaddy has ever been in one, either. Even though I'm running so late, today is still going to be a beautiful day, and I'm still going to write those letters.

CHAPTER TWENTY

I can't write home. I can't write home. I can't write home about the air show. I never made it there. Maybe I should have just never tried, because the whole thing went wrong starting with what happened last night. I did get up and go, anyway, and I made it to the top of the hill but not even down the other side. Not even to the next McDonald's after the one nearest us, right at the end of the hill. I was going to stop there to go to the bathroom. I have been practicing the hill for a few days, and today I made it to the top. You would think going down the hill would be easiest, and it usually is, but a group of boys can ruin anything.

There is this funny thing that I do to get myself up the big hill and even up some of the smaller ones. Because my bike is so old and beat up—it really is, even though I did a good job at fixing it up—it has a hard time climbing hills. I have to stand straight up on the pedals and talk to my bike to get it to go. That's what I say, "Go, go, go, go, go, go," until I get up the hill. I say it out loud to make my legs, and the bike, work harder. So I am doing this and I'm almost there and cars are blurring past me, but it doesn't matter because I am enough on the shoulder that I'm out of the way. Then I feel a car slow down and guess they are trying to be polite—trying not to scare me. I wish they would go on, but I keep pedaling up. *Go, go, go, go, go.*

Whoever is in the car is having a great time laughing, and I can hear that it is not women and it's not old people. For a half a second I look back and see three or maybe four boys laughing.

"Go, go, go, go, go! Where you going?" one of them shouts.

Then the same thing happens to me that happened when I saw the robbers take Marie-Bernard's purse: my eyes and my brain separate. I see what is going to happen and my brain acts like it is gone, like the scarecrow in *The Wizard of Oz*. Nothing there.

I watch one boy, a cute boy, lean way out of the car. I hear him tell his friend, "Slow down." And then, "Move over some." When I look at him, right in his face, he just smiles at me; he even says hi. Dumb me says hi back.

The thing is, he looked sweet, like somebody who no matter how much other boys were mean, would never be mean himself. More than that—he looked like the kind of boy who would never let any of his friends act mean, either. It was because of the way he said hi and looked right at me. I think he was actually looking for my eyes.

I kept pedaling and kept wishing they would go on by me. I was ready to get to McDonald's because I needed to pee, and I was getting thirsty, too. "Nice ass," was all the sweet boy said. Then he leaned out as far as he could and he grabbed my nice ass. Before I could even tell what he was doing, my body knew, because it was on fire where he was holding me. I kept pedaling, and he kept holding me, and truly, that part of my body was burning up as if I had sat down on the hot eye of a stove. His friend sped the car up, and me and my bike went dragging along with them, and the sweet boy was still holding on.

"Goddamn, my goddamn arm, slow down," the sweet boy said to the driver.

"Man, just let go of her," said the driver. I heard them arguing about this—whether to slow down or to let go of my bike—while I was tumbling down the hill. I watched my bike somersault down the hill three times. The basket got smashed, and the wheels got knocked out of line so that the handlebars pointed all the way left when they should have been pointing straight ahead.

I think that I must have just been in a daze, because it wasn't until I had walked my bike back to our building that I realized I was bleeding in a lot of places. Both of my hands were scraped up, and one of my knees was just a little bit red, with some pieces of gravel stuck in it. But the other knee was gushing with blood. My white sneaker and sock on that foot were already red, and the blood was what I would call pouring out of my body.

What I had thought this morning was that I looked really cute today. I was comfortable that I just looked like a girl, not like anybody that anybody would want to bother. I had put on my gray sweat shorts and a navy blue golf shirt and my Panama City baseball cap. Now grass from the side of the road and tar from the pavement covers my shorts and the backs and sides of my thighs. I can't find the key to our apartment. It's not around my neck,

147

it's not in my sock, and it's not in the pocket of my shorts. My daddy is not home, since on Saturdays he works two shifts in a row. I am glad that he won't be home until the middle of the night, but I want to be inside. My head is hurting so loud. Both my elbows are stuck full of gravel.

I go to Marie-Bernard's and pound on the door. Marie-Bernard is always telling me, "Us women, we need to stick together." I pound on the door again, hoping she will answer and I can tell her everything. She will fix me a cup of strong black coffee with lots of sugar, like she always does, and tell me that everything will be okay. Then I remember that she and J.J. took a bus to Miami to visit Marie-Bernard's sister who has come to visit from Haiti. A lot of Marie-Bernard's relatives live in Miami, and they all bug her to move there, too, but Marie-Bernard won't go. She says Miami is no good as a place for J.J. to grow up. I don't ever tell her this, but this building here in Jacksonville is not so hot a place, either.

So I just stand here trying hard to look normal in case someone comes by. I'm sure there is something I can do to get in, but it's just not coming to me, the something that will get me inside. There are bars on the outside of all of the windows. I have no key. Marie-Bernard is not home. I could call my daddy to come home, but I wait for another solution to pop into my head.

Tamika comes in and starts to turn her eyes away from me as usual, but she just can't do it, because I am bleeding so much and because I must really look like something is wrong.

"Oh, my goodness, are you all right?" she asks.

"Well, I think so. I just had an accident on my bike, and I can't find my key."

"Where's your boyfriend?" Tamika asks me.

This doesn't make any sense to me, because I have never had a boyfriend and I don't even know any boys here.

"Who?"

"Your boyfriend. The guy who lives here with you." Tamika says this like I'm an idiot.

"Oh. He's my daddy," is all that I can say, and I'm wishing that Tamika had just kept on ignoring me forever.

"Jesus. Are you for real?"

When she asks me this, it's like my body just can't hold me anymore. I start to cry, loud, in the hallway, and worst of all, I pee in my pants, partly because I have been holding it for so long. I am crying, peeing, and bleeding in the hallway with Tamika. She lets me do this for a couple of minutes without interruption, and I must need it, because the crying doesn't stop after the pee; it just gets worse.

"Come on, let's get you upstairs and clean up that

knee," says Tamika, and she puts her hand under my elbow and takes me into her apartment.

It is beautiful inside, and cleaner than anyone's house I've ever seen. Even Nana, who cleaned all day every day, never kept her house sparkling like this. There is no dust anywhere, the trash cans are all empty, and she has real flowers on the dining-room table. At this moment, I am the opposite of Tamika's apartment; I am as filthy, almost, as a person can get. This doesn't bother Tamika one single bit. She tells me to sit on the couch while she draws a bath for me.

The tub is one of those old-fashioned ones with animal feet, and it's as deep as my shoulders when I sit down. She fixes the bath perfectly hot so that it doesn't burn me, it just exhausts me. Tamika takes my clothes, hands me a washcloth, and leaves the room. It's funny, but I am not at all embarrassed to be like this with her. I have known her, really, for about fifteen minutes, and she has seen my naked body getting into the tub, but I don't mind. In fact, I am relieved to be here. I soak in Tamika's bathroom for an hour or maybe more. Every time the water cools off, I add more hot, and I cry until the tears come out empty, like the dry heaves you get when you're really sick. It feels good especially to cry hard for a few minutes and then float my whole body under the hot water and lie still as dust with the washcloth over my face. I'm not thinking about anything. I'm just thinking about nothing.

CHAPTER TWENTY-ONE

When Tamika finally comes to get me out of the tub, she knocks on the door and asks, "Are you a raisin yet? May I come in?" That's funny that she calls me a raisin, because Nana used to call me a raisin, too, when I soaked for a long time. Tamika comes in with two things for me: a fluffy white towel that is taller than I am and a fluffy white robe.

"Here, dry yourself off and then come out here and let me look at your knees." She is tender in a way that reminds me of how Granddaddy Tate is when the fishing hook gets caught on the seat of my pants. It's hard to explain how that happens, except I think I must have a bad habit of letting my line out while the fishing rod is behind my back, before I cast. He never loses patience and always untangles me in such a quiet, soft way that I never feel silly or embarrassed. That's how I feel with Tamika putting ointment on my knees. She wipes away the dirt, and the ointment goes on without my even feeling it at all.

Tamika makes the most delicious and pretty supper that I have had since Nana was alive. When she said she was fixing fish for supper, I got kind of excited at the thought of catfish. Instead, she makes a spicy baked salmon. She serves wild rice and asparagus together with the fish, and it is all arranged on the plate like a picture. She frames the meal, around the rim of the plate, with a sauce drizzled to look like the latticework that our climbing roses at home use to grow up. Tamika drinks a glass of wine with her meal. Well, she drinks about three glasses of wine. But that doesn't bother me.

At home, nobody drinks—I mean, none of my family. I know there are some people who drink—such as Mrs. Parsons, Ginger's mama. But those who do are real private and secretive about it. Take Mrs. Parsons, for example. The only reason I know she drinks is because Ginger showed me a six-pack of Budweiser wrapped in a brown paper bag, hidden in the very back of the icebox.

She also showed me some wine tucked away in a box in the bottom of her mama's closet. Ginger was showing off when she showed that to me.

Here in Jacksonville, all the people sit right outside on the stoop and drink their beer as if it was nobody's business. At home, you could get in real trouble for drinking in public. For one thing, Tippah County is what is called a dry county. That means there's a law that says absolutely no alcohol allowed, not in the stores, the restaurants, or even people's houses. I have heard, from Ginger, that some people keep cooking sherry and giant bottles of vanilla extract in their cupboards in case they need a quick drink. You have to drive all the way to Middleton, Tennessee, before there is a store that sells alcohol. Here, every restaurant sells all kinds of liquor and beer and wine. The restaurants that I'm used to only serve ice tea, lemonade, and coffee. Some of the fancier places might also have Coca-Cola or Sprite.

During supper, Tamika and I have a nice talk about lots of different things. I tell her all about Nana and Granddaddy, and she tells me all about her work. She tells me, "Eat up—you're wasting away to skin and bones. We need to fatten you up a little. You're a growing girl." Just her saying that makes me feel like I am already halfway home.

"God, I hate assholes." That's what she says after I tell her how I wrecked my bike. I tell her about the sweet boy, the one who grabbed me, and she nods, like she agrees that really sweet boys can do dumb stuff and it's not really their fault.

"Why don't you hang out here until your . . . dad gets home? I've got to get dressed to go to work, but you can stay here and read or sleep or whatever you want."

"Thank you, Tamika. Should I sleep on the sofa?"

"Where do you sleep downstairs? All these apartments have only one bedroom."

What happens to me here is awful. I do sleep on the sofa, but I understand that her question isn't about sleeping, really, and my face turns red as her lipstick. I can't look at her, but I say, "I sleep on the sofa." And it's true. But I start to cry and end up telling Tamika everything. I tell her about my nana dying and my mama not really being dead. I tell her about Sissy making me strip in the driveway and my daddy making me dress up and wear trashy clothes. I tell her about slow dancing and driving my daddy home. And then I tell her what he did to me last night.

There is a part of my brain that tries to stop me from telling everything to a complete stranger. But there is a bigger part of my brain that thinks it is time for all of this to stop and for me to go home. That part of me thinks Tamika is a helper, just like the Good Samaritan who picked up the beaten-down traveler and took good care of him.

After I have stopped telling her everything, and after I have finally stopped crying, Tamika says in a quiet and true voice, "Don't worry; you're safe here with me. Tonight, get some rest, and tomorrow we'll figure out what to do. Have you ever slept on a waterbed? There's nothing like it in the world; come on."

She shows me to her room, and I am falling asleep while she's telling me when she'll be home. She's beautiful, way more beautiful than I look even when I dress up for my daddy. Her hair is in a perfect twist in the back, and she is wearing a black sleeveless dress. It's linen. I only know that because she told me three times: she loves linen, this dress is linen, and linen is supposed to wrinkle. That's how you know it's linen. The linen is perfect on her, and even though she is talking about loving wrinkles, I know that Tamika won't come back with a wrinkle on this dress. Her earrings and necklace are pearl. I don't ask if they are real, because I think that would be tacky and also because everything else in Tamika's place is real. The flowers are real, the linen, the leather on the sofa—all real. Even the bubble bath is in a crystal bottle. The pearls are probably real, too. Her shoes are plain black heels, and she doesn't wear black stockings the way Daddy likes me to; her stockings are just skin color.

"Tamika, can you make me look like that?" I hear myself saying as the bed is wrapping me up in its rolls.

She laughs and says, "Sweet dreams." Then she asks, "Did your nana ever sing you to sleep?"

I tell her that my nana sang the sweetest song I've ever heard—a lullaby about Christopher Robin.

"My mother used to sing me a song like that."

And then she sings the exact song to me:

> "Little Boy kneels at the foot of the bed,
> Droops on the little hands, little gold head;
> Hush! Hush! Whisper who dares!
> Christopher Robin is saying his prayers."

I fall asleep easily, and I dream of my nana. In my dream, she is rounder and pinker than she ever was in real life, and she is waiting for me outside of a room that is full of people and every imaginable good thing to eat. I smell chicken, rolls, apple pie, and other things I don't recognize. I hear music and people laughing and calling to her: "Lucy, join us!" She turns to go and I beg her, "Nana, please, may I come with you?" All she says to me is, "No, sweet child, not this time." I call out to her, "Wait!" and she turns back to me and holds me close to her for a long

157

time, but not long enough. "I love you, Georgia Tate. You're my precious girl." Then she is gone. I am awake.

When I wake up to go to the bathroom, I'm totally confused about where I am. I know it's not home, and I know it's not the sofa. It feels friendly, but my mind can't find anything that happened before now. It does know where the bathroom is. In the living room, I see a white sofa that I know is not my roach-and-flea-infested sofa. Someone is curled up there, a woman with a little blanket over her feet. It's Tamika, still in the black dress. When I see her, my mind has everything back in place and I feel a little, or a lot, sad. I remember that Nana is really gone. I remember that I miss my granddaddy, and I remember that I want to go home.

Tamika is sleeping hard on the sofa, and it seems like it would be ruder to wake her up and offer her own bed than to let her sleep more. I could sleep forever. It's almost three-thirty in the morning. I know that down-stairs, underneath the waterbed, my daddy is at home. I did not leave him a note because I hadn't planned on spending the night with Tamika. I hadn't planned to lose my key or get knocked off my bike. I hadn't planned, either, that he would do that to me in the bed.

CHAPTER TWENTY-TWO

It's been three days since I wrecked my bike and that I've been staying with Tamika. I have only left the apartment once, to visit Marie-Bernard and J.J. after they got back from their visit to Miami. Marie-Bernard is going to move to Miami, after all. I guess she just couldn't resist the pull of being near family. I can understand that.

For an awful lot of my time at Tamika's I have been sleeping—and eating. Tamika doesn't keep a scale anywhere in her home, so I can't say for sure, but I think I am already starting to gain back some of the weight that I had lost from not eating all summer. Tamika is a good cook, but different from the kind of cook my nana was.

Nana made everything she cooked from the recipes in her mind. Just about all of her dishes came from what she learned to cook as a girl. Sometimes, if a friend would bring some new and yummy dish to a church meal, Nana would ask for the recipe and add it to her memory.

Tamika, on the other hand, cooks from recipes out of fancy magazines and cookbooks. She said she loves having me here to cook for, because it's hard to cook special meals for just one person. One night she made six teeny tiny chocolate soufflés. That was kind of different, but tasty. They were little bitty, so I ate four of them.

I called Ginger, and I told her what has happened since I came here. I told her that I am too embarrassed to tell my granddaddy myself. Ginger is going to call me back at Tamika's since I'm not staying downstairs anymore. Tamika invited me to stay here until I can figure out how to get home. She just came right out and said, "Georgia Tate, I'd like you to stay here with me for as long as you want." I think that's the nicest thing anyone has ever done for me—opening their home and their heart for no other reason than to help me out of a bad spot.

Tamika thinks we should call the police on my daddy. What she said exactly is that because my own daddy did those things, it is even worse than if a complete stranger had done it. Tamika thinks he should go to jail. I don't know how I feel about sending my own daddy to jail, or even about calling the police to tell them. Plus Tamika said that the police might take me from her apartment and put me with some other nice people temporarily. I don't want to stay with anybody; I want to go home, even though telling my granddaddy everything will be harder than telling the police.

Even during the daytime Tamika looks like a girl, except for her body. I watched her do her makeup this morning. Her eyebrows are not real; she draws them in with a brown pencil. She said she can't go anywhere without her face on. That makes me laugh because she goes everywhere with her head up in a bandanna, and in one of those wrinkly African-looking skirts. At night before she goes to work, she looks almost like someone's glamorous mother, with her makeup and clothes perfect. But in the day, when it's obvious that she is not one hundred percent girl, Tamika looks out of place with herself.

Tamika smoked four cigarettes, one right after another, this morning while she did her face. She didn't ever smoke an entire one, but she'd let them burn and then take long drags while she tried to get her eyebrows right. I think she is chain-smoking because of her nerves. I mean, she is happy to have me stay here, but I can tell the thought of the police busting in is really getting her worked up. Especially because my daddy has figured out where I am. I guess it wasn't that hard to figure out.

Last night, after midnight, he came up to Tamika's apartment all drunk, pounding on the door and shouting for me to come out. He told me to get my ass downstairs. I didn't even answer the door or go to it. I just sat on the floor in the kitchen and listened to him hollering.

Tamika was at work when he first got here. When she got home, he was still standing there but not shouting anymore. By that time he had gotten to the part where he talks all sweet about being sorry and wanting to make it up to me. She didn't start anything with him; she just said, "Excuse me, sweetheart, you're blocking my door." The amazing thing is that he let her walk right in past him, without even trying to get inside. He just stood there and said, "You tell Georgia to get home. I'm calling the cops if she's not down here in the morning." Tamika didn't say a word back. Then I heard him call Tamika a faggot.

She found me on the floor in the kitchen. I had to crack up laughing because when she saw me, she turned on the kitchen light and squatted down and held her hand out to me and said, "Here, kitty-kitty, it's okay now."

That is what is so great about Tamika. She is too sweet to ever ignore somebody's hurt. I think if my mama had a friend like Tamika, I'd have more than just a letter; I'd have a real mama, and maybe none of this would have ever happened.

Tamika's job is at a dance club downtown where they have shows called drag shows. Tamika does the girls' makeup and arranges the costumes, and she also sells Mary Kay cosmetics. That's where the money is, according to Tamika. She is always saying, "Mary Kay products pay the rent and keep me beautiful." I am witness to the fact that the only beauty products she uses are Mary Kay products.

Most of Tamika's makeup comes free from Mary Kay—either as a prize for selling so much or as a sample to try before she sells it. Tamika says she has a client base of close to a thousand girls, only most of them are not really girls. "Client base" is just a fancy way of saying regular customers. She has regular customers all over Florida and all the way up to Atlanta. She goes to different drag shows, doing makeup and costumes. Some of her customers call by telephone to order every week.

Tamika says that I am too young to wear any makeup at all. That is just like Nana. Ginger's mom lets her wear makeup, but Ginger is almost a year older than I am. Even though Tamika is against my wearing makeup, I convince her to give me a full beauty makeover, just like in the magazines. She starts out with a facial that is called a deep-cleaning mud mask. We leave that on for twenty minutes. Then she cleans my face with something called astringent. By the time we get to the makeup, she has used at least six different Mary Kay products on me. She smokes even more cigarettes while she does my makeup.

It is no wonder that so many people buy only from Tamika. She makes you feel like you're already beautiful. For one thing, the Mary Kay smells good and feels good. The main thing, though, is that Tamika is an expert at making it seem like you don't need a thing other than your own God-given beauty. All the while, though, you are thinking it's Tamika, and the Mary Kay, making you beautiful.

When she applies the moisturizer with just her finger-tips, she says, "Your skin is so soft and pure. I'm going to use a very light touch, as if I were drawing with a pencil." Or when she puts on the eye shadow she says, "Let's bring out how blue your eyes are. They are gorgeous. I'm going to apply white directly under the brow and this light beige on your lids. Very subtle, you don't need much." I admit I feel like a beauty queen when she is all done.

After the makeover, Tamika makes me clean my face with Mary Kay cold cream. "Now, remember this when you turn sixteen. Moisturizer first, then light eyes, light lips, very light blush. But no makeup until then. And if I catch you wearing makeup before then, I will wipe it off myself."

She is teaching me to play backgammon, but it just doesn't suit the way my mind works, so I'm not very good. I always win whenever we play Scrabble. I can really put some words together. The other night I put the word *maize* down on a triple word score; it was the *z* that made it great. Tamika did not know that *maize* is what the Indians called corn. I've known that forever. I got it from Nana. She once scored a triple word score with *maize* and beat me good. I have been trying hard to get a triple word score with *maize* ever since then. The only thing that is not great about my Scrabble game is that I can't seem to get higher than 400. I have come pretty close in the past week with a 375 and a 385 game, so I think 400 is coming soon.

Ginger called back this morning, just like she said she would. On the phone, I told her all about Tamika. "Ginger," I said, "do you know what a drag queen is?" I was pretty excited to tell Ginger about something like drag queens. We don't have any at home, so I'm sure this is new to her. I don't even bet there are any drag queens in the whole state of Mississippi.

Ginger hasn't hardly ever even been anywhere. Her

idea of going someplace big is driving to Tupelo with her mama and shopping for school clothes. There is a store in Tupelo that has the most beautiful clothes in the world. In fact, at about this time every summer, Nana would take me there to buy two new dresses, one for school and one for church. Other than that, Tupelo is just not much to brag about. But, boy, do they ever brag about themselves, because Elvis was born there.

According to Nana, Elvis told people he was from Memphis before he ever lived in Memphis. The house he was born in is still there in Tupelo, and they charge way too much just to walk through it. Well, I'd never pay it. The house is rinky-dink, and you can just stand on the front porch and see the entire house through and through. That is not a lie. It's that small. All of the McDonald's in Tupelo are even decorated in Elvis stuff.

Tamika loves Elvis, and I think she also would love Ginger. Most folks don't know what to do with Ginger, and I think those same folks wouldn't know what to do with Tamika, either. I will say one thing, though: I don't think anyone who is a friend of Tamika's has ever felt embarrassed or shameful about anything at all around her. It is impossible for me to think badly of Tamika, even though a lot of people probably think her way of living is just flat-out wrong. The truth is, Tamika is good as gold, and I'm sorry that more people don't know this about her because we could all use what Tamika gives—that feeling of being okay just however we are.

This morning, Ginger asked could she tell Granddaddy Tate everything for me. I just said, "Okay." I cried like a baby after we hung up, and Tamika held me tight for a long time.

CHAPTER TWENTY-THREE

Today, I helped Marie-Bernard pack up and get ready for the move. While I was there, my daddy came upstairs to Tamika's with a police officer. It is just a stroke of luck that I was not there. I heard them in the hall and then looked through the peephole of Marie-Bernard's door. Tamika opened her door to let them both inside, and they were in there for a long time, I suppose looking for me. Marie-Bernard and I took turns watching through the door. When he left Tamika's, the policeman said for Tamika to call if she heard from me. My daddy kept saying that Tamika was lying, and that he knew I was in there somewhere. I admit I was a little nervous that Tamika might tell the police everything right then. But she didn't.

Then the officer turned to Marie-Bernard's door, and I ran fast into her bedroom and hid in the closet, praying that all of this would not be real. From the closet, I heard the knock at the door, and then the officer said he wanted to ask Marie-Bernard some questions. I was so afraid, I was nearly shaking. But Marie-Bernard proved that she is as good a friend as there ever was. When she told me before that women need to stick together, well, I see now that she sincerely believes that.

Every question the policeman asked, Marie-Bernard answered in Creole—that's what they speak in Haiti. I couldn't hear what exactly he was saying; I could just hear the sound of his voice. I think he was getting right frustrated, because I could hear him talking louder and slower. She just answered him louder and slower in Creole. Finally, I heard the questions stop and the door shut, but I stayed in the closet for more than an hour. In fact, I didn't come out of the closet until I heard Tamika's voice real low. I came out into the living room, and everybody looked as scared as me. Then Tamika handed me an envelope from Western Union. I am going home.

My granddaddy wrote me a telegram saying to come home right away and that he was sorry he made me go.

He also said that he is going to court to get custody. He already talked to a lady lawyer. What he did was tell a lawyer about what I told Ginger, and the lawyer said, with just that and nothing else, my granddaddy and me would win in any court in the country. I've been reading what Granddaddy wrote over and over again. He said my daddy is going to be in big trouble, but first I need to get home. It's nice to be saying *get home,* instead of thinking about going someplace strange.

He sent me three hundred dollars—way more than enough for me to get home. It is enough to buy a bus ticket and still have some money for food and things if I need it. I tried to give Tamika some money for being so nice to me and letting me stay with her, but she wouldn't let me do it. Not one dollar would she take.

All I have to say is, thank goodness my grandaddy finally figured out that he is really my daddy. Maybe he figured it out one day when he was sitting in the truck at Green-Old-Field, thinking of my mama. Grandaddy Tate is the one who made me a sandbox when I was little. He built me a swing set. He took me to town to get my first Bible. He taught me to fish. He taught me to drive. He taught me a lot of things, and he looks at me in the right way.

That whole time—the time of me being born, and my mama shooting herself—must have been a time of our family being ashamed. But not one day of my life at home did I ever feel ashamed of myself or of my mama. My granddaddy did that for me. He just never did give anybody permission to be embarrassed or quiet or whispery about me. I rode around with him on his visitations to the hospital and the nursing home. He took me with him to the square, and every time I met somebody new, he would say, "This is my granddaughter Georgia Tate. We're real proud of her." He was, too. I could always tell that.

Another thing different about Granddaddy from my daddy is that Granddaddy listens to me think and likes to hear what I have to say about all kinds of things. I think he even learns from me, too. Even about his own specialty—God—Granddaddy listens to me about that.

Once, a while back, when I was still living there, I asked Granddaddy what he thought about lady preachers. I was always bugging him about lady this and lady that. He reminds me, when I get a little impatient with him being backward about girls, that women couldn't even vote when he was born. The world really has changed on him, and he mostly does a good job of understanding it all. I have to give him credit, because he is not used to women doing what they're good at and what they like, especially when it's something not many women have done before. Most all of the churches at home are against women being preachers.

"Granddaddy? What do you think God thinks of lady preachers?" was how I asked him the question, just plain out, right like that.

"Well, I don't know any lady preachers personally, but the way I look at it is like this—who am I to tell God who He can or cannot use to spread the Gospel?"

I thought that was the smartest, truest answer I've ever heard. Nobody can really argue about that. In fact, Granddaddy went on a right long time about Paul, in the New Testament, sending a lady named Priscilla to preach the Gospel. I told him that I thought even the Easter story itself says it's OK for women to preach.

"How so?"

"Well, who was the first person to tell the good news about Jesus being alive?"

"Mary Magdalene."

"Right. So if she was the first to spread the Gospel, she was the first preacher, right?"

"I can see that."

"And Jesus didn't just accidentally bump into her on His way out of the tomb. He was already out, and He came up to her, didn't He?"

"Yes, He did."

"Then you could even say He picked her, out of all the men and women who had been following Him around all the time, to be the first to see Him. And not only did she see Him, but He also told her, 'Go tell everybody what you've seen,' right?"

"Yes, I think so."

"Well, there you go. It was the plan from the beginning. First Mary Magdalene, and then Priscilla."

"Georgia Tate, I believe you have a gift. Do you think about this sort of thing a lot?"

I just nodded and went off to meet Ginger. The truth is that I always think about this sort of thing, and I never do. What I mean is that I never sit down and think about this apart from anything else, separate from the rest of me. It's all mixed up together inside, and usually it comes out when I am talking with Granddaddy. It will be better than all the ice cream, new dresses, or bike rides in the world to just sit and talk with Granddaddy Tate like that again.

CHAPTER TWENTY-FOUR

At the bus station, it's just like having my family send me on a long trip. To others, it might look like a strange family, though. Marie-Bernard and J.J. are here, too; their bus to Miami leaves a little bit after mine. Tamika drove us all over; she is weepy because she's going to miss me. She looks good, though. I would've expected her to dress up if we were going to the airport, but even for the Greyhound station, Tamika has really gone out of her way to look real nice, better than anybody I've ever seen even at church or at a wedding.

She's wearing linen for the last time until next year. I learned from Tamika that you should stop wearing white and linen after Labor Day. She is wearing a pale pink linen suit with white high heels. She is even wearing a little hat to match her outfit. Her hair is done up real simple, and what impresses me the most is that she is wearing gloves. Tamika is straight out of a movie. Everyone can't take their eyes off of her—one because she looks like a Hollywood star; two because she is so far past crying, she is sobbing; and three because me, Marie-Bernard, and J.J. are tagging along behind her while she figures out where I need to be and everything else.

Marie-Bernard and J.J. are dressed up, too. Marie-Bernard is still wearing her yellow bandanna, but she has on a new purple dress and purple shoes to match. J.J. is wearing a light blue suit with a navy blue bow tie. He looks like a miniature old man.

I am nervous that I will get on the wrong bus when it's time to change, or I'll fall asleep and miss the stop at New Albany. I know the bus station in New Albany isn't really a station; it's just a grocery store with a bench outside. I have seen it before, but I've never been on a bus before.

Tamika and Marie-Bernard went in together to buy me a new journal and a real nice writing pen. It has blue ink; they know that I much prefer it over black ink. The journal has lined pages inside, and the outside is black leather. It's almost too beautiful to write in, but I know that a twenty-hour bus trip will give me lots of time on my hands.

Marie-Bernard also gives me a Saint Christopher medal; she said he is the protector of travelers. And she gives me a little statue of Mary, Jesus' mom. She calls this statue Our Lady of Guadalupe.

Tamika gives me two Mary Kay products: lip balm and facial lotion. Tamika believes in keeping your face moist all the time. She said being on a bus will dehydrate my skin, so I should use it often.

There is one seat left on the bus—an aisle, not a window—and it's next to the biggest black man I have ever seen in my entire life. As soon as I sit down, he starts making friends with me.

"Hello, Miss, I'm Leroy Bennett. May I ask your name?"

"Georgia Tate Jamison. Most everybody calls me just Georgia Tate. How long will you be on this bus?"

"I'm going to Booneville, Mississippi, so I'll be on this bus until Birmingham, Alabama. There I change buses to get me to Mississippi."

I cannot believe that Mr. Leroy Bennett will be on the same buses for the same time as I will. I think that he must be an angel sent for the sole purpose of escorting me home. I can't help but smile real big at him.

"I have a daughter about your age, I think. She's turning thirteen next month. I haven't seen her in three years."

"I'm still twelve," I say, and I'm wondering why he hasn't seen her.

"She's named after me because she looks just like me."

"You named your daughter Leroy?"

"No." And he says this next part serious. "I named her Leroya."

Well, this makes me laugh out loud. Leroy Bennett laughs out loud, too, at me laughing out loud at him.

"It's nice to see a girl laugh so big and hard, but what is so funny, please?"

I can't even get a word out to explain myself, so I just shrug.

"Well, G.T.—that's what I'll call you for short, okay? Leroya is the feminization of Leroy. Is that so funny?"

"No, that's real nice," I say. "I bet your daughter will be happy to see you."

For a long time Leroy Bennett and I sit together without saying a word. One or the other of us keeps looking up like we want to talk but don't know what to say. We are already agreed-upon traveling friends, so I try to start something up.

"Three years is a long time to not see your daughter. Have you been riding buses that whole time?" He looks

177

at me full in the face, and then he just lands the whole truth right on my lap.

"No, G.T., I've been in prison most of that time. Accused of armed robbery. Can you handle knowing that and riding this bus with me?"

"I guess so."

"Okay, well we won't talk about where either of us have been lately, only where we are going. How about that? A deal?

"Deal."

Mr. Bennett is also a poet. I know this because he is carrying a notebook that says in block letters on the front: LEROY BENNETT, POET. PRIVATE! KEEP OUT!

Leroy Bennett is as black as night. Darker than Marie-Bernard, darker than any person I have ever seen in my entire life—darker than anyone at home, or in Tupelo, Florence, or Jacksonville. I am looking at him, thinking that if I were a lightning bug, it would be hard for me to resist blinking on and off because he's so dark.

We don't talk for a long time; we just ride the bus together, and we both write a lot. He won't read his poetry to me because he says it's too angry and that he can tell I am too broken to handle all of his anger. He also says that I'm too young. I am a little relieved inside to hear this, but I say, anyway, "That's okay—I can probably handle it. I can handle a lot, you know." I am almost begging him to read me something even though he doesn't want to, and he gets a little upset with me.

"G.T., life is two things: it's terror and it's joy. My poems are the terror. I put the anger to words and write it on paper so that I don't harm anything or anyone, including myself. My poems are real good—but they are for me only. They are the only thing of my own that I have."

"Oh," is the only thing that I know to say about this, because he's right. I feel that about my diaries, too; that they are only mine. And Mama's letter, too. She kind of says the same thing that Mr. Bennett is saying, that your feelings can't really hurt you if you look at them and accept them. I feel more embarrassed about bugging him so much to read me his poetry than when Ginger's mom caught us watching the turtle crawl across Ginger's titties. He doesn't seem bothered, though. He explains, "Writing poems like mine would do you no good. Now, if you wrote about joy, that could heal you."

He says this to me as if he already knows every thought and picture and word that has ever hurt me. I think again that he must be an angel, because only angels know everything about a person, I think.

"I don't think I can," I say. "Joy doesn't last as long as terror, does it? It doesn't last long enough to remember."

This makes Mr. Bennett laugh so hard that the old woman with the big red hat in front of us turns around and glares at him. Mr. Bennett laughs louder and says to the woman, "Laugh with me, ma'am. It's a long ride to Birmingham." The lady in the hat doesn't laugh with him; she just snorts a little and turns back around.

Birmingham is when we will finally change buses and can get out and walk around for a while. Even though it will be the middle of the night when we get there, everybody is looking forward to having a chance to stretch and to get something to eat. For Mr. Bennett and me, we both can't wait to use the telephone.

Then Leroy Bennett says, "I disagree with you about the shortness of joy. We have a long day ahead, so let's play a game. What is the most joyful smell that you know of? Quick, without thinking!"

"Honey buns and coffee coming from Nana's kitchen on Saturday mornings."

"How about the most joyful sound?"

"Umm . . ."

"No. No *umms*. Quickly, tell me a joyful sound heard by Georgia Tate."

"My granddaddy singing 'Amazing Grace' to himself. No. A mockingbird, singing every bird song she knows, really fast in a row."

"And the most joyful feeling?"

"Feeling like heart-feeling, or feeling like touch-feeling?"

"You're stalling for time. Touch."

"Aunt Mazel's long, silky hair in my hand. Now your turn," I say. "What's the most joyful smell that you have ever smelled?"

"The smell of my wife's skin in the morning before she wakes up and showers."

"The most joyful sound?"

"The sound of cows in the field talking to each other after dark."

"And the most joyful touch-feeling?"

"My daughter's hand holding tight to mine."

"What's the most joyful heart-feeling you've ever known?"

"Freedom. The feeling of getting on this bus and being free to go home."

"Me, too."

We play the joy game forever and talk about songs, memories, trips, everything we can think of that is joyful. He has two rules about this game. One, you can't stop to think—you have to say the first thing that pops to your mind—and two, you can't repeat anything. The goal, he says, is to discover that joy is easy to find within yourself. It goes on and on like a rainbow does.

I like the joy game. It does make me remember feeling good, and I guess that is the first step to making the joy last longer than the terror. I remember feeling good with Nana and Granddaddy Tate when I was little, before this summer started. I remember it, and I plan to always remember it so that I can find my way back. That was before I started getting a chest and growing private hair. Before I started making Nana think about Mama. Before I ever knew my daddy again. I imagine that's me still—the girl who ran around the garden, catching frogs; who could sprawl in the grass, looking up at the sky until it was time for lunch. I keep thinking: I have been there before, and I can get there again.

CHAPTER TWENTY-FIVE

Mr. Bennett is by the window, not me. That is the only real complaint I have, besides how cold it is on this bus. So far, Mr. Bennett has sat by the window for the whole trip and has not once asked if I'd like to. When we stop again, at a big town long enough to get out, then I will ask him to trade spots with me. He is asleep right now, with a pillow against the window. I brought my favorite pillow, but there's really nowhere to put it.

It's funny to look at Leroy Bennett while he is sleeping. In his face, he looks probably just like he did when he was ten. He looks only about that old. And it's almost like looking at a little boy sometimes, even when he is awake. I wonder, when Mr. Bennett was ten, did he ever think he would get put in jail for something somebody else did? I believe him that he didn't do it. Because I can see sometimes that people don't care who gets in trouble for something as long as somebody does.

Mr. Bennett's daughter and wife did not see him the whole time he was in prison because they could not afford to go down to Florida. I don't know how Mr. Bennett ended up from Booneville all the way to Jacksonville, Florida. He said he came down to Florida to look for a job and was planning to bring his wife and daughter later.

"But that turned out real bad," is all he says to me about how he came to be a jailbird. "And now I'm going home."

I wonder if everybody in Booneville that's kin to Mr. Bennett is happy for him to be home. I think that he is a good man. I hope that his family and his daughter are at the grocery store right now buying everything that they need to have a big dinner in just his honor. That would start things off right for him.

I hope my granddaddy and Ginger are doing the same thing for me, making plans to celebrate. Even if it's just the three of us, I want to go home and know when I get there that it's the right place to be. I will call Granddaddy Tate from Birmingham just to make sure he knows exactly when this bus will be pulling into New Albany.

Leroy Bennett, the dark black poet, is awake now. Even though he has scooted way over toward his side of the seat, his arms and legs still spill over to my half of the space. He is wearing real faded blue jeans, a gray T-shirt, and a black leather vest. He also wears a Saint Christopher medal. It is big, way bigger than the one that Marie-Bernard gave me.

"Hello, G.T.," Leroy Bennett says to me. "Looks like we're about there. Would you care to join me for breakfast in Birmingham?"

I have never had breakfast at four in the morning before, but we will be here for almost an hour, and I am hungry now that I'm awake. Mr. Bennett orders two breakfasts: eggs, grits, biscuits, and juice, and then pancakes, sausage, and coffee. He eats every bit of it, too, and drinks a whole pot of coffee.

I love breakfast food and have a hard time deciding, but the picture of the French toast looks so full of cinnamon that I have to have it with a lot of butter and syrup and sausage links. There is a choice, at this restaurant inside the bus station, of sausage links or sausage patties. I always go for links over patties, and I am surprised that they have both; usually, it's one or the other. I don't drink any coffee, so maybe I will sleep the rest of the way and won't be so tired when I get there.

After breakfast, Mr. Bennett and I make our phone calls home. It is too early even for Granddaddy, but I don't care. I know he doesn't, either, because he doesn't answer the phone, "Hello"; he answers it, "Georgia Tate?"

All I can say is, "Hi, I'm almost home." We go over it a couple of times that I will be in New Albany, at the Big Red Grocery Store, at eight. He tells me, more than one time, that he will be there at seven, just in case we are early. My granddaddy doesn't want to hang up from talking to me, and neither do I.

"Well, how is the trip? Are you doing okay? Have you met anybody nice that you can talk to on the bus?"

I tell Granddaddy all about Leroy Bennett, even that he is a black man who used to be in prison. This part I almost leave out because I can see Nana standing over me pursing her lips tight at the thought of me hanging around with a black man—only Nana would say "nigra." I decide to tell Granddaddy because he knows me now, and I know him, and there is nothing that I want him to not know.

I even tell him that although Mr. Bennett was in jail for three years, he thinks about things in the same way that Granddaddy and I do. All of this Granddaddy Tate understands. "Georgia Tate, you can make friends easier than anybody I know. Mr. Bennett sounds like a real nice traveling companion, and I look forward to meeting him in New Albany."

Granddaddy also tells me that Aunt Mazel is there, waiting for me. She is going to stay with us for as long as we need her to stay. I need her to stay forever, but I reckon we will get to that later.

Mr. Bennett has started me thinking about family and what it means. I am thinking that my granddaddy is my family. Ginger counts as family, too—and Aunt Mazel. They know me the best, and I believe how much they love me is real. So right there, talking on the phone to Granddaddy Tate at four in the morning, I decide that I will love him and let him love me back. That's why I tell him all about Mr. Bennett and me, writing poetry and songs, and both of us restless to be home soon.

We start to hang up, and my granddaddy's voice cracks real bad when he says to me, "Georgia Tate, I called the Jacksonville police today. Everything is going to be all right now. They want to speak with you, of course—that might be hard, dolly—but don't worry; we're going to be just fine together." Then he doesn't say anything for a second, and we both wait for the other one to talk. "All right, then. I love you."

"I love you, too," is what I say, and we hang up.

I wanted to ask him some questions about my mama, but I will save that for when we are home and can be face-to-face together. It will be better that way. In a face-to-face meeting about something this important, we'll be there to help each other after the fact, when we're most likely to need it.

There has never been a happier day than this one, except maybe tomorrow.

When we get back on the bus, Mr. Bennett and me are both too happy to sleep. He talked to his wife, his mother, and his daughter. Even though Mr. Bennett lives in Booneville, he'll get off the bus at the New Albany stop—just like me. He said his wife, Elsie, sounded real happy, and they are planning a fine dinner to welcome him home. Mr. Bennett even invited Granddaddy Tate and me to come over to Booneville and join them.

My granddaddy didn't say anything about planning a big dinner, but that's A-OK with me. I imagine that we will sit together and eat some fish. He has probably been catching fish, just for when I get home. We will probably ask Ginger and her family to come over, and I'm sure that a bunch of people from church will stop by to visit.

Everybody in town knows that I'm coming back to be with Granddaddy. Dr. Ellis, the preacher from Holly Springs, is coming to preach for Granddaddy today, so he can be with me all day. We will probably do a lot of visiting people and eating. School starts on Tuesday, so there is a lot of planning and getting ready to do between now and then. Even though we won't go to Booneville for dinner with the Bennetts first thing, I did say that one day soon we could come for a visit.

"Elsie and I would really like that. Your granddaddy Tate sounds like a fine man—a real man of God. I would like to meet him."

"You will love him, Mr. Bennett, and he will love you. Both of y'all are alike, you know."

"How's that?"

"Well, you both care about the truth—him in a quiet sort of way. You both care about your family, and though not everybody knows it about my granddaddy, I think you are both brave enough to stand up for what is right, though it takes Granddaddy a while to get straight about what to do."

"Is your granddaddy straight now?"

"He sure is."

"About what?"

"I think after all of this, he is straight about everything—about me, about my mama, my daddy, my nana. You know, about family and staying together. I think he is different now; he is talking like he's not afraid of what anybody thinks. He's talking like he's free, too. I know he would be happy to come to Booneville with me, and I don't think he always would have done that."

"That's a gift you gave him. He decided that he was going to love you with his whole self, and he is opening up to be the best father to you any girl ever had."

CHAPTER TWENTY-SIX

Right as soon as we pull into the bus stop at the Big Red Grocery Store in New Albany, I can tell something is wrong. My granddaddy is not there. But Ginger is there with her mama. They are all dressed up like they're going to church, but it's eight o'clock in the morning, and church is a long way off. Even Sunday school doesn't start until ten. I am hoping that maybe they came real early, and we're all going to get breakfast together—except my granddaddy is still not here.

Leroy Bennett must can tell something is wrong. He

is shaking me on the shoulder real gentle-like. "Georgia Tate? Georgia Tate, what's wrong, girl?"

Before words even reach my brain to come out, I know there is something scary coming next. But I push that knowledge way down and walk up to Ginger and her mama, trying to be real happy about seeing them and wanting to get a straightaway answer to the big canyon in my stomach. I kind of see, but more can feel, Mr. Bennett right beside me, and that helps me feel not so alone right at this very moment. There is a part of my mind that watches Mr. Bennett hold his hand up to somebody across the parking lot, telling them to hold up a minute. I see a real pretty girl and a lady who must be her mama walking over. They are dressed up, too, like they're going to church at eight in the morning, as well. "Hey, Ginger. Hey, Mrs. Parsons, I mean Mrs. McCann. Where's my granddaddy?"

For too long a second, nobody says anything, and everybody's standing around staring at me except Ginger. She is pushing gravel around with her shiny Sunday shoes and looking down at the ground like she's about to crawl into the earth. Poor Mr. Bennett looks like he wants to say something but can't find a single word.

Ginger's mama's face is all crinkled up, and her mouth is kind of frozen in an O like she's having trouble with words herself.

"Where's my granddaddy?"

"Where's my granddaddy?" I hear myself saying this over and over until finally Ginger's mama says, "Sugar, I've got some bad news. Brother Tate was in a bad car accident on Highway 15, near Green-Old-Field, early this morning, and they took him to Tupelo not even an hour ago."

"Tupelo?" I hated to hear Tupelo. When Nana died, they didn't take her to Ripley; they took her to Tupelo. Here's the truth. They only take people to Tupelo who need special attention. People who go to Tupelo probably are not going to make it. When that Bragg boy was in an accident, they didn't take him to Ripley; they took him to Tupelo, and then he died. There are more doctors and nurses and special equipment in Tupelo. And if you ask me, more people don't come home from Tupelo, either. About the same second as I am thinking all this, Ginger pipes up, having to be Miss Dramatic and Miss Know-It-All, and says, "Georgia Tate, they ain't sure he's going to make it."

I can't breathe, it is so hot. My chest hurts, and I am so filled with fear that I can't move. All around me it looks deep and black as night. I want to cry, but I am not a baby. So I haul off and punch Ginger Parsons so hard in the mouth that her lip starts spraying blood all over her nice Sunday dress. Before I know it, Ginger and me are fighting like two boys in the gravel and I'm winning. She's more or less just trying to keep me from making any more contact with her body, but it's not working.

It's Mr. Bennett who pulls me off. "Come on, girl. This young lady didn't hurt your granddaddy. Get up off her and let's get you to Tupelo."

"Excuse me, but who are you?" says Mrs. McCann. "And what makes you think you're taking Georgia Tate anywhere? Sweetie, you come on home with us now."

I just ignore her, but I'm thinking to myself that I will punch her in the mouth, too, if I have to. I say, "Mr. Bennett? Would you really take me to Tupelo? Can you really do that?"

"Friends take care of each other, G.T. Just like your friend Ginger here is trying to do in her own way. Of course we'll take you."

Ginger is still sitting there in the gravel and dust. Her pretty dress is ruined, and she is covered with blood. "You going to Tupelo with a colored man? Are you crazy?" she says from down on the ground. "Mama, you letting her go?"

I can tell Ginger's mom doesn't know what on earth to do. She looks scared to death and like she—like every one of us standing there—was hoping she could rub her eyes hard enough and all this would just go away.

Mr. Bennett's pretty wife steps in closer to us and says

to Ginger's mama, "Don't worry; we'll take good care of her and be sure she gets to see her granddaddy. We'll have her call you when we get to the hospital." This seems to make Mrs. McCann feel better about things, having a woman around to watch over me.

"Georgia Tate, one of the deacons took your aunt Mazel up there shortly after the accident, so you be on the lookout for her. And you call us. Lord, I hope this is the right thing to do."

Mr. Bennett tried to introduce all of us and make polite conversation on the way to the hospital. I did remember to tell them thank you, over and over again. Thank you one time did not seem to be enough. They were real nice to me, even Leroya, and I thought it was awfully generous of them to give me Mr. Bennett on his first day home of freedom.

CHAPTER TWENTY-SEVEN

The body is there for sure. It's hard to tell if much more of Granddaddy is in this room or not. All the tubes and machines hooked up to his body, and not one of them can tell me if he is still in there. Aunt Mazel sits right beside him, reading her Bible to herself. Without checking, I know my gold-lettered Bible is waiting for me in my backpack.

Marie-Bernard always calls a backpack a knapsack. That's what Nana called it, too—a knapsack. I really don't understand why. *Knapsack* makes no sense at all.

Backpack does, because that's what it is—a pack you carry around on your back. Backpack. My backpack is the very one that my granddaddy had in World War II. He was in the navy—a chaplain, not a sailor.

I can tell by looking at Granddaddy and Aunt Mazel that there'll be a lot of praying in this little room. I kiss my granddaddy on the forehead and whisper right into his ear, "I'm home." I want to say to him, "I love you," but instead, I decide to wait until I know that he's in his body and can hear me. Right now, I figure he is off talking to God, and maybe Nana, about what to do next—to go home to heaven, or to come home to Ripley with me.

I wouldn't want to stop my granddaddy from being with God, if that is where he decides he wants to be. But more than anything—more than having Nana back, more than finding my mama, more than wishing I had never socked Ginger's face—I want to go home to Ripley with my granddaddy.

Outside, it's raining. I can hear it really pouring now, and even though the shades in Granddaddy's room are pulled shut, the light coming in is the light of a cloudy day. Mostly I love days like this. I feel so protected and wrapped up tight by the clouds and rain. Today I feel hushed—like God is hushing me until all this about Granddaddy is figured out. If the sun even peeked a little bit, it'd be like giving us all permission to be hopeful.

Aunt Mazel is still sitting in the only chair in this room. Usually, when Aunt Mazel reads her Bible, she likes to do so aloud, drawing everybody into the story she's on at the moment. Today she only looks up every now and then to say, "Your granddaddy loves you, Georgia Tate—you're all he has left." Truth is that we're all each other has left—me, Granddaddy, and Aunt Mazel. That's enough to make a family.

What I want to do is to finish being a little girl, and then when I'm all grown-up and can take care of myself and my own family, then I want to take care of my granddaddy, too. I want my own little girl to go fishing with him. And then, after all of that, if he needs to go to God, then it will be all right. But it's not all right for him to go now.

Coming back here to live with Granddaddy, I knew that someday it would be like this. Meaning that I'm not a dummy—meaning that the ending, of course, would someday be a whole lot closer than the beginning. But not today—the ending is not supposed to be today. Today is supposed to be the beginning.

Aunt Mazel is reading from somewhere in the Old Testament; I can tell because she is reading from the front of the Bible, and the New Testament is more in the back. Sometimes God gets so mad in those Old Testament stories, but usually not in what I call the girl stories, like the one about Naomi and Ruth, Naomi's daughter-in-law. That one is a story that makes me cry every time I think of it. Ruth just followed Naomi around, like an old dog that's been with you forever.

I think that's how I am with my granddaddy. He sent me away, just like Naomi tried to send Ruth away. But now he's Naomi, and I am just like Ruth; I am not going anywhere. I bend close to his ear again, even though I am pretty sure he is somewhere else at the moment. He doesn't have his hearing aid in, so I make my lips touch his ear and I say to him:

> *"Wherever you go, I will go.*
> *Wherever you live, I will live.*
> *Your people will be my people,*
> *and your God will be my God, too."*

I want to say *I love you*. But I am waiting until I know that he is here with me.

In the blur of all of this, I halfway see Mr. Bennett whispering to Aunt Mazel, and her nodding like she understands. I just can't make myself leave Granddaddy's side.

After a little while, Aunt Mazel hands me a note and says, "Your colored friend has left you this." I had forgotten all about Mr. Bennett. I didn't even have the right mind to say bye or thanks or anything. I am hoping he's not mad and that I will see him again; that after all of this, Mr. Bennett and I will stay friends. I think how nice it would be if between us we could find a way to be a part of each other, even though Ripley and Booneville are not going to be exactly the easiest places to try a mixed friendship.

The note doesn't say anything except his phone number. And he signed it: *Your friend, Leroy Bennett*.

Aunt Mazel is watching me; I can feel it on my neck. "He left me his phone number. In case I need anything, I guess," I tell her.

"That's what friends do, Georgia Tate; they look after one another, right?" she says.

I'm glad Aunt Mazel is ready to talk, because I'm ready to talk, too.

"Aunt Mazel? Is it right to ask God for specific things?"

"Like what, hon? Well, sure, if you are asking with a pure heart. In other words, you ain't asking for a fur coat because you're jealous of somebody else's coat or because you want to show off. Then sure, if your heart is pure, then I think it's your job to ask God for everything you want. Everything!"

"I wasn't really thinking of a fur coat."

Sweet Aunt Mazel wraps her arm around my waist and tells me, "I know."

"I want to ask God to let my granddaddy come home to me, not Him."

"All right, then ask Him."

"Now?"

"Now sounds good."

I look at Granddaddy, who still only looks like an outline of himself. So I take in a deep breath, and I don't worry too much about getting all of the words right. Out loud I say: "Please help me. I came all the way back to start all over again—this time with my granddaddy and me. Please, can you let him come home with me? Can you let him be okay? Thanks a lot."

"Okay," I say to Aunt Mazel.

"Okay what, sugar?"

"Okay. I asked."

"I heard. I think you asked very nicely, too."

"Well, now what?"

"Well, now we wait for God and your granddaddy to work it out between them."

"Just wait?"

"Yes, just wait. Or, you could sing."

Aunt Mazel calls singing making joyful noise. Joyful noise; I like that. My granddaddy always sings, too. He and Aunt Mazel both seem to spend a lot of their time singing—mainly hymns. For no reason at all, they sing; I guess they just like to do that. My granddaddy especially likes to sing "Amazing Grace."

I think about curling up in the hospital bed and singing to my granddaddy. I am a little nervous from all of the cords and tubes, so I just press up to his ear again and start singing, "Amazing grace, how sweet the sound / That saved and set me free. . . ." Aunt Mazel is standing right beside me and rocking back and forth.

"Louder," she says.

"Was blind but now I see. . . ."

"Keep singing! Don't stop!"

"Through many dangers, toils, and snares / I have already come. . . ."

I sing the whole song, three times over. Somewhere in the middle, a nurse comes in, too, and she and my aunt Mazel start singing with me. I kiss my granddaddy and notice for the first time that he still smells like himself. I smell him again. I breathe in hard that outside, sweaty smell he always has on his neck. There is one tear gathering up in a pool, between his eye and nose. I kiss him again and whisper directly into his ear, "I love you." Outside, the rain keeps falling. It is a good rain.

GIGI AMATEAU says of her character Georgia Tate, "We have a lot in common. We're both from Mississippi. We both love catfish, watermelon and rainy days, and our granddaddies saved our lives – mine when I was fifteen and in a lot of trouble, and hers when she was twelve and far away from home. Georgia Tate has taught me so much about hope, family and claiming the life that is yours." Gigi Amateau lives in Virginia, USA, with her family. This is her first novel.